Dedalus Europe
General Editor: Timothy Lane

EVERYBODY
DIES
IN THIS NOVEL

Beka Adamashvili

EVERYBODY
DIES
IN THIS NOVEL

translated by Tamar Japaridze

Dedalus

This book is published with the support of the Writers' House of Georgia and Arts Council England.

Published in the UK by Dedalus Limited
24-26, St Judith's Lane, Sawtry, Cambs, PE28 5XE
info@dedalusbooks.com   www.dedalusbooks.com

ISBN printed book 978 1 912868 82 7
ISBN ebook 978 1 915568 19 9

Dedalus is distributed in the USA & Canada by SCB Distributors
15608 South New Century Drive, Gardena, CA 90248
info@scbdistributors.com   www.scbdistributors.com

Dedalus is distributed in Australia by Peribo Pty Ltd
58, Beaumont Road, Mount Kuring-gai, N.S.W. 2080
info@peribo.com.au   www.peribo.com.au

First published by Dedalus in 2023
Everybody dies in this Novel copyright © Bakur Sulakauri 2018
Translation copyright © Tamar Japaridze 2023

The right of Beka Adamashvili to be identified as the author & Tamar Japaridze as the translator of this work has been asserted by them in accordance with the Copyright, Designs and Patents Act, 1988.

Printed and bound in the UK by Clays, Elcograf S.p.A.
Typeset by Marie Lane

The Author

Beka Adamashvili

Born in 1990, Beka Adamashvili is a postmodern Georgian author, blogger, screenwriter, and Creative Director at an advertising agency. In 2011 he graduated from Caucasus School of Media at Caucasus University with a BA in Journalism and Social Sciences.

In 2014 his first novel *Bestseller* was published. It became a real bestseller in Georgia and was on the shortlist for the best debut novel at the SABA Literary Awards and as the best novel at the Tsinandali Awards. It also received a special prize at the Iliauni Literary Awards.

In 2018 Beka Adamashvili published his second postmodern book *Everybody Dies in this Novel*, which won an EU prize. Both books have been published in English by Dedalus.

The Translator

Tamar Japaridze

Tamar Japaridze is a highly acclaimed Georgian translator and academic. She was the winner of the SABA Literary Prize in 2016 for the best translation of the year.

She has translated over thirty literary works from English into Georgian, including authors such as William Shakespeare, Rudyard Kipling, Harold Pinter, John Fowles, Henry Miller, Arundati Roy, Irvine Welsh, Bernardine Evaristo, Margaret Atwood and Kazuo Ishiguro.

She has translated *Bestseller* and *Everybody Dies in this Novel*, for Dedalus.

Prologue

Death set his alarm clock for 4:33am.

He had been counting everything since insomnia became his vigilant adversary. First he counted the sheep (ten thousand one hundred and ten!), then the sleepless nights (seven thousand seven hundred and seven!), then the seconds spent on counting the sheep and the sleepless nights (eighteen thousand and three!), then the seconds spent on counting the seconds spent on counting the sheep and the sleepless nights... suddenly, it struck him that there were six hundred and twenty(!) other ways of falling asleep besides this futile counting, and he decided to try something else.

He thought, he'd better think about nothing, but then realised that thinking of thinking about nothing was already a thought, and felt a persistent ache in his cranium. Next, he turned to a volume by Proust hoping to fall asleep from boredom, but soon reckoned that it wasn't worth his while, as he didn't want to be in search of lost time later. Neither closing his eyes to all injustice nor imagining the public reading of the Tokyo telephone directory was of any help. In the end, he waved his wrist bones and finger phalanges despairingly, stared at the wall opposite, and tried to calm himself down by the fact that, all in all, his state was far better than that of the Devil who had never once slept in all his days...

...The opposite wall represented a part of Death's cozy but pretty dead office. On the left there was a door with a huge poster of Jim Morrison – his favorite lead vocalist, a worthy member of his precious collection that was still incomplete. He wanted his collection to consist of twenty-seven unique specimens. When all the twenty-seven were there, he would create the best music band of all time, with big names, equally big performers, and the sequels (such as "Also Like, Haha and Wow" or "Five more months, please".[1]) to hits of different epochs. But the valuable specimens had to be selected with the accuracy of a jeweler, since the increasing number of willing applicants threatened the quality of the future band.

From the corner of the room, right where two walls met, there started an exhibition of myriad wonderful photos (eight thousand seven hundred and forty-five in total number!). All of them depicted him, and the whole thing represented a sort of a summary or rather a chronicle of 'Death at work'. The remarks inscribed on the edges of the pictures gave a detailed account of his lifetime activities – *A Time to Live and a Time to Die:*

---

1 The sequels to the hits "All You Need Is Love" and "Wake Me up When September Ends".

A huge scythe hung on the third wall. It hung diagonally, on two nails. After new technologies had been introduced, Death scarcely utilised it as intended; he mostly used it as a selfie stick or a prop (he was always depicted holding the scythe, you know, and he didn't want to deceive the expectation of mortals). He was no longer a kid, so to speak, and was tired to death from carrying the scythe on his shoulders. However, he had a scythe-shaped cursor on the monitor of his special device from the company ATROPOS, in which he kept numerous (seven thousand four hundred and twenty!) subfolders ('War', 'Cataclysm', 'Disease', 'Accident', 'Old Age', 'Terrorism', 'Crucifixion', 'Darwin Awards', etc.) and seven billion eight hundred million five hundred thousand three hundred and twenty files (fancy that!) in a huge folder named 'Humankind'. His job was to distribute continuously updated files into

9

subfolders and delete some of them from time to time.

Over the 'ATROPOS' there were shelves full of Terry Pratchett books. To Death's mind, Terry Pratchett used to write unforgettable books, until he had to be sent to the 'Alzheimer' subfolder. Some other novels, too, were written very skillfully by famous Authors: Mann, Zusak, Saramago, Christie and many others who tried to acquire immortality by writing about Death, and hence helped to revive his narcissistic library.

Death rubbed his eye sockets (which were staring at the wall) with the thumb and index finger phalanges. His insomnia was caused entirely by psychological factors. He was afraid to fall asleep with fatigue so hard that even the alarm clock could not wake him up. "I must consult a psychotherapist ASAP", he decided. The last one he visited in 1939 was Freud. But he didn't consult him, it was just his duty visit, since the file 'Sigmund Freud – 1856' had long been in the subfolder of 'Severely Sick,' and it was already the poor man himself who was lying on the couch. "Never mind", Death calmed himself down. "He was good at discussing sleep, not sleeplessness". Then he recalled that his insomnia occurred much earlier than his visit to Freud, namely after one occasion when he had to be very vigilant but fell asleep, and the world's entire history changed dramatically.

Alois was to die during coitus. By all means! Otherwise, the experiment would fail, and Death would be strictly accused of inefficiency by his creators.

That evening Alois drank everything but deadly poison. Acutely intoxicated by alcohol, he even suffered from diplopia: one finger seemed to be two to him, those two seemed four, and four seemed eight. Eventually, it

resulted in such an anatomic abnormality, that the poor man had to close his eyes and shake his head to come back to reality. For the same reason, upon returning home, he (having at last found one real door out of sixteen) first saw one Klara, then two, then four, and then eight respectively. So, he closed his eyes, shook his head, and before his wife multiplied again, he took her to the bedroom to multiply the number of his family members.

Their coitus was nothing like the sex in romantic movies; it was more like the act of reproduction in documentaries from the series 'Animal Planet': Alois puffed like a train in the movies by the Lumiere brothers, and Klara was as silent as the same films.

The lethal heart attack should have started at that very moment.

But alas! Death fell asleep.

A fatal misfortune indeed!

Several minutes later, the act was over and Alois, panting heavily, climbed down from Klara to the bed. At first glance, this was an ordinary night like one thousand and one other nights, but it turned out to be fabulous: wee Adolf defeated his enemies using the blitzkrieg tactics and headed towards his mother's ovum at the speed of light...

...The unpleasant memory not only kept Death fully awake but also made him lose the desire to think about sleep whatsoever. He stood up, took off his cloak, and examined himself thoroughly in the mirror. "I need to gain weight, I am nothing but bones", he concluded. Having hung his cloak over the electric chair, he began to think about coveted holidays. He really deserved a good rest after millions of years without a single day off. "Of course, *He* doesn't care... *He* himself rests on Sundays, anyway", Death grumbled, and suddenly spotted someone in the dark... damned hallucinations! He rubbed his eye sockets with his finger phalanges and scrutinised the darkness in front of him. This time he saw no one there. So, he chilled out, lay down and continued to meditate. Time flew quickly indeed! He remembered Abel very well, as if they met just a century ago. Death was a simple intern those days, and it was too difficult for him to get used to his job... aw, and how he sweated while chasing Methuselah... then there came that Great Flood. He worked forty days in a row, but one tippler – a carpenter – spoiled his every effort. Recalling the Flood reminded him of the "Titanic". It was awfully cold that night and Death was chilled to the bone... brrr... he shivered. Once he witnessed a devastating heat in London: September of that autumn was so hot as if it was on fire... when the image of the blazing fire submerged into the fluid of his subconscious, some new images emerged from it by the principle of buoyancy... Archimedes... a hot bath... together with Marat... the warm water felt very pleasant... the sudden feeling of pleasure thrilled the whole of his skeleton. He relaxed.

"I must not sleep!" he thought, and fell asleep almost instantly.

It was about four in the morning.

Another Prologue

As Memento Mori awoke one morning from uneasy dreams, he discovered that he was a fictional character, and that he remembered only three things about himself:

1. He had a strange name – "Memento Mori";
2. He was a fictional character;
3. He remembered only three things about himself.

It's difficult indeed to be a character in such an odd situation, especially when you appear right in the prologue from nowhere, knowing nothing about your past or future, and being able to say only a few words in three short phrases about your present. You are surrounded by strange void spaces: if you go to the window and look out of it, you might see vast emptiness. Moreover, you won't be able to spot the window at all, if the Author doesn't say that the room, in which you happen to be, has four large windows with a wonderful view on the rye field over the crazy cliff, and that the whole of this spot is especially beautiful in the late autumn, when the tree branches resemble gigantic brushes, while leaves look like the drops of coloured paints.

The author should also say something like 'it's a wonderful experience to watch *heffalumps* and *woozles* floating by the south window', and so on and so forth. But the thing is that Memento Mori won't go to the window, as he thinks that description of the nature is always pretty unnatural. By and large, he thinks that one living tree is much more important than the whole forest described on many pages for which the very tree has been cut down. Anyway, let me remind you that Memento Mori still doesn't know anything about what he knows or thinks apart from what has already been said about him. Neither does he know what will be said further.

And yet, unlike him, the majority of characters usually never realise that they are characters, and that even their simple decisions, such as *what to have for supper*, for instance, come from another person's mind. There is nothing extraordinary in such naivety. Imagine a stranger coming up to you and asserting that actually the Earth is nothing but a fictional planet from a book by an inhabitant of the planet *Kimkardash*,[2] and that in reality you, too, don't exist either. Would you believe it? You wouldn't, of course.

As for Memento Mori, he first found out that he was just a fictional character and only after that he believed it. In the world where a human being can turn into an enormous insect in his sleep, or where a huge black cat walking on two legs can ride a tram hanging on it, nothing is impossible. "However," Memento Mori thought, "if the Author always directs the character's thoughts, then it might be his decision as well to make me think that I can act independently. Therefore, my sense of senselessness of such a character might also be dictated by him"…well, well. What's the use of worrying about such trifles when by accepting the idea that you are a fictional character, you acquire a great literary power: you can make the other characters rebel against the Author, completely ignore his words, or just travel from book to book. So, tell me, for goodness' sake, who cares whether it all happens at the will of the Author or not? No one does! Neither will Memento Mori. The Author has died! And the literary critic who first asserted this fact died as well. So, Long Live the New Character!

***

Three asterisks in a row usually stand for the phrase 'time has passed'. That is to say, nothing important happened in Memento Mori's life between the last line of the previous paragraph and

---

2 Kimkardash – a fictional planet in a book by an inhabitant of the planet Earth.

the first line of the following one. He only slept and ate. As nobody feels like reading about the characters that are only sleeping and eating, Memento Mori decided to exchange his laziness and drowsiness for something more impressive. He had an exclusive superpower, let alone everything else, and ignoring this fact (especially in the world full of cruel Authors who could kill their characters with one simple sentence) was the same as to forget the password of your own WI-FI. Such an unfair situation needs one superhero at least – Supermento! Mementomori-man! Termimentomori!!!!

Or let it be Memento Mori again.

For several years (which might sound a long period of time, but it can be described in fifteen letters, as you see) he had been reading various books from 'The Sense of an Ending' to 'The Neverending Story'. Then he started skipping from book to book making an effort to save protagonists: he tried to assure Romeo and Juliet that there was no need to turn every problem into a tragedy, because later their problem might seem merely a sweet memory of the past. He also tried to offer the first aid to Ostap Bender while Ippolit Matveyevich was drowning in a river (Bolivar Cannot Carry Double).[3] At times, when the magic penicillin had been already invented, he even visited the Davos sanatorium in secret. Sometimes he managed to triumph over the Authors, but some other times the length of the book created a serious obstacle for him, and struggling through its pages he missed the train of the protagonist. Once

---

[3] Bolivar Cannot Carry Double – the purpose of this insert is to indirectly demonstrate that the Author knows one of the stories by O. Henry. Therefore, do not pay attention to this footnote, despite the fact that this comment is in the second part of the statement.

he even tried his luck with *War and Peace*, but surrendered in no time. He wasn't able to save the Lisbon girls from *The Virgin Suicides*, neither could he succeed with ***Spoiler Alert***[4]... what could he do? He was dealing with a million other characters all alone. Little wonder he couldn't manage to save them all, (and there was no need of doing it by the way). He even pushed Moriarty himself at the Reichenbach Fall, and still remembered the bewildered face of Sherlock whose razor-sharp mind could not guess from where this *deus ex machina* came.

Frankly speaking, travelling through the books didn't prove to be exciting either. True, it was much better than a continuous process of eating and sleeping, but several more paragraphs, and the reader (fed up with so many literary allusions) might close the book with such a sound and fury that Memento Mori would be crushed between its pages. The only way to avoid such a terrible misfortune was to start telling a *new story*... at that very moment, Memento Mori found out something that saved him from the Sword of Damocles: while he was concerned with other problems, someone's murder had been planned in his own book. The murder had to take place in the morning, at 4:33 sharp!... yeah, everything was written clearly in the prologue, except one detail:

Who was to be murdered?

---

4 I mean Randle McMurphy, whom Memento Mori couldn't save, although (unlike Ken Kesey) he at least tried to.

Sorry, You are Condemned to Death!

Spoiler # 1: Ernest Hemingway is a Murderer

"Close your eyes and imagine that you've been given a superpower to eliminate one person from world history. Who could it possibly be whose absence would thoroughly change everything?" Professor Arno took his eyeglasses out of his shirt pocket and set them on the desk instead of on his nose. "As a rule, it's Adolf Hitler who comes to one's mind, isn't it?... if anyone has other candidates, we can discuss them straightaway."

The audience obviously had some other candidates, but had no desire to discuss them. So, the Professor concluded that the majority shared his opinion and went on more boldly:

"I wonder why Hitler became a figure in world history – was it really because of his remarkable moustache or due to his famous gesture, which is now used solely for hailing a taxi? Maybe the swastika proved to be the perfect logo? Or should we blame his charisma for everything that first caused a storm of changes and then a powerful hurricane of armed conflict hitting the entirety of Europe?"

"Maybe because of the large numbers of those killed,"

suggested a 'Mr. Know-all' from the depth of the auditorium.

"Not likely! If we measured someone's greatness by the number of their victims, then a monument to Mao Zedong would have been erected on a pedestal greater than the Great Wall of China! 50 million more people fell victim during his regime, but I don't remember any discussions about how world history would have changed if some time-traveller had gone to the small Chinese village and killed newborn Mao…" Professor Arno took the glasses from the desk and (as the description of characters' actions and movements between phrases seemed to him a meaningless obstacle to the unhindered flow of narrative) decided to stand still till the end of the lecture. "…whereas various story plots of the kind have been invented about Hitler. In one of them a Holocaust survivor, a Jewish scientist invents the time machine to kill baby Adolf; in some others the mature Adolf is liquidated, but a new leader replacing him conquers the entirety of Europe; still in others the alternative development of history is determined by Hitler's victory itself, or simply he is not rejected from the Academy of Fine Arts and persists in painting the rest of his life, creating canvases of 'no artistic value' instead of the disastrous prospects for mankind."

"And would the war still have broken out if Hitler hadn't been born? I mean, can the situational factors cause more changes in history than certain individuals?" asked a male in a Che Guevara T-shirt sitting in the front row.

"Much has been said and written about this matter", Professor Arno admitted pausing to fit his glasses. "Let's put it this way: if the *Führer* was merely the individual who happened to be in a certain place at a certain time, how come that when Hitler, and for instance, Franz Ferdinand[5] or Gavrilo Princip[6] are described in books, only the identities of the last two need clarification in the footnotes? Is their conscious or unconscious role in starting World War I less important? No, of course not, at any rate at first glance. But the difference still lies in 'situational factors' and 'certain individuals': if Gavrilo Princip hadn't been born, someone else would have killed Franz Ferdinand or his substitute... that's to say, the situation in Europe of those days was pretty tense, and declaring war was always going to happen even without Princip. As for World War II, frankly speaking, I can't imagine it without Hitler. His role as a specific individual in changing the history of mankind is almost indispensable..."

Professor Arno, who was 'Arnold' in his passport and referred to as Mr. Arnold at his bank, had been dreaming of changing history since his childhood, but the only thing he managed to change was his dream. He chose the profession of archaeologist, and all his youth he was a chaser... umm... chasing after the skulls and skeletons of HOMO-SOMETHINGs with a couple of remaining teeth and the frames that were not attractive at all. He had been digging for twenty years in a row, but his most important discovery was the fact that everything of great importance had already been discovered. As a result, he buried his dream deep in the ground and was spending his remaining days searching for alternative ways of getting into history.

---

5 Franz Ferdinand – Archduke of Austria-Hungary, whose assassination by a Serb student Gavrilo Princip precipitated World War I.

6 Gavrilo Princip – a Serb student who assassinated Archduke Franz Ferdinand of Austria-Hungary, which precipitated World War I.

To put it more expressively, *infiltration into history became his idée fixe.*

"Actually, humans cannot change history; they simply make it. If you want to change it, you should either become a historian..." Professor Arno adjusted his glasses recalling the words similar to those of a certain French writer: "...or travel back by time machine and, for instance, force Hitler to give up his *Kampf.*"

"Yes, but..." someone protested, and having already uttered the phrase 'yes, but' was obliged to go on: "...haven't the scientists already proved that it is physically impossible to travel back in time?"

"And I can prove right away that any scientist can be wrong!" Professor Arno didn't know what else to do with his glasses that wouldn't seem too hackneyed; he was already fed up with fishing around for rare verbs describing his movements. "Years will pass, and it will be *impossible* for humans even to imagine what might be *impossible* for them."

From his own experience he knew that the trite device of repeating one and the same word – 'I'm *confused* that nothing can *confuse* me', 'I *apologise* for *apologising* very rarely', 'I'm *afraid* of only my own *fearlessness*', and the like – was the simplest way to prove himself witty, and never missed a convenient moment to resort to it.

"Moreover, are you sure that the period of time we find ourselves in right now – this public lecture, I mean – is not already history? Are you certain that we are the first in this time-space continuum? That no one has come before us, and that "tomorrow" has not arrived yet?

Someone shrugged his shoulders but no one, including

himself, noticed it.

"Let's imagine that we have invented a time machine and visited, say, Van Gogh…"

Having heard the name of Van Gogh, a girl in the third row with dark circles under her eyes smiled warmly and became starry-eyed.

"Here, look at Vincent! He is standing in his room, stained with paints all over. Painting his sunflowers, he is quite sure that what is going on there is in the present, that there is nothing beyond that day yet, and that the 21st century is as far away as his acclaim… but we – people 200 years after him – can assure him of the opposite. True, he won't lend us an ear and will consider us crazy, but then…"

"The Doctor will put him into the TARDIS and take him straight to one of Van Gogh Museums."

"Doctor who?" Professor Arno inquired and instantly decided to search Google for that word – *TARDIS* – as soon as the lecture was over. He always felt very miserable when someone knew something he didn't.

"…Well, it doesn't matter anyway… I was only trying to say that right at this moment, someone, who is two centuries ahead of us, can possibly be delivering a lecture saying: *maybe two centuries earlier, an elderly professor stood at this very desk and spoke about Van Gogh who lived four centuries ago.*"

Several listeners in the auditorium decided that Professor Arno was the cleverest person they had ever heard. A lot of people in the city shared the same opinion, which really puzzled the Professor himself, for his public lectures were not distinguished by profound philosophy or high competence. Despite this (or, maybe, because of this), he never complained about the small numbers in the audience. Moreover, sometimes he was even paid a substantial sum of money for repeating something he had already said one thousand and one times for free.

"But time machines would cause the greatest collapse in history…"

…The legal ways of entering which Professor Arno had been seeking in vain for the last decade. He excluded war from the very start, since he didn't seem to have been born for the role of an army commander. As regards entering history collectively (like 'Famous War Heroes', '300 Spartans' etc.), it didn't appeal to him. Setting some outstanding temple on fire was also excluded – firstly, because plagiarism was not a proper thing for a scholar, and secondly, because choosing that path would most likely lead him to prison rather than making history. He even tried to go in for politics, but before he managed to change anything, his government itself had been changed. In the end, when the source of his imagination had thoroughly dried up, he decided to prepare an impressive final speech to imprint his name forever in the memory of posterity.

Or, to put it more expressively, *to make his mortal speech immortal!*

"Can you explain in plain words the principle by which the time machine works?"

"Well… we'll return to this question later…" Professor Arno used a standard answer to prevent discussion on a topic he knew nothing about. "…but one thing I can say for sure: maybe time travel seems a miracle to us now, but history proves that a "miracle" is a synonym for a "prospect." Today you cannot surprise anyone with the drawings of a submarine or by transformation of water into wine; miracles seem to be out of date – no one believes in them if they are not captured on photographs or on videos; even if they are, everyone thinks that this must be just a good fake…"

No miracle had ever occurred in Professor Arno's life. He didn't even have a single interesting experience that might be worth telling his grandchildren… moreover, he didn't have any grandchildren either to whom he could tell tales. The world balanced everything perfectly. So, the main thing was simply to turn all those phrases and words that he had never uttered within the framework of the perfectly balanced world into a perfect final speech. It had to be brief, smart and heart-rendering like one of the inscriptions on the wall of a concentration camp: **If God exists, he will have to beg for my forgiveness.**

Or, to put it more expressively, *he wanted to create a slogan that would summarise his life…*

"Did you know that all this centuries-old history was written in advance?" Professor Arno was just leaving the university building when he heard the words of a stranger. He was wearing a Che Guevara T-shirt, and both of his eyes were of the same colour[7] – kaleidoscopic. "…Yeah, all this is a mere fiction. We are simply participating in an experiment, where you might be condemned to death."

Professor Arno was certainly sure that he would die someday, but he was not planning to die that soon. He was so confused that in response he could recall only one of the

---

7 **Both eyes of the stranger were of the same colour** – an allusion to Bulgakov's famous novel, which would be devilish hard to recognise without this footnote.

phrases that might be used as his final sentence:

"Death does not scare me, since I greatly doubt that being in Hell is worse than staying on Earth."

Spoiler # 2: Professor Arno Is Grabbed by a Billboard

It was not enough for Matthew to stop the wonderful moment passing away; he wanted to freeze the entire time: the faces of the clocks, their hands, alarm ringtones, even hand-timers, calendars, and poor cuckoos. True, he was not Rick Sanchez, Dr. Faust or someone more intellectual... let's say Joshua of Navi,[8] but still. It was high time that one had thought seriously of getting hold of time.

Yet Matthew's methods were not perfect. Initially, he decided to go to bed late and get up early to gain at least five hours per day. It continued until he looked like an extra in mass scenes from *The Walking Dead*, and was forced to seek better ways of achieving his goal. It was then that he got rid of all clocks and watches at home, as they were 'a direct declaration of time flying'. But soon he realised that there were clocks everywhere around as the city didn't want to waste time guessing what time it was. He even tried to introduce the effect of expectation and filled out new lottery tickets immediately after the previous draw, so that time dragged on endlessly

---

8 **Joshua of Navi** – the leader of the Israelites and simply a good guy. He asked God to stop the sun in its course when he was waging war against Canaanites, and God fulfilled his wish without any problem. That's it – you will get anything you wish if you have someone to pull strings for you!

while waiting for a potential million. Naturally, he couldn't gain a million, and even more so the time. Finally, he decided to take a long-term loan from the bank, since the loan had one paradoxical principle – the days passed too quickly from month to month, whereas they lasted endlessly from year to year. But alas, even though time is money, money didn't prove to be time! In short, Matthew realised that he was wasting time thinking about how to save it. So, while he still had a little time, he switched to new ideas... however, he had far more ideas than time:

- He wanted to open a shopping centre named 'Judah' with the slogan WE SELL ONLY THE BEST!
- He wanted to create several identical minimalistic canvases with different titles:

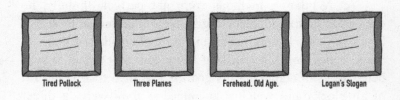

Tired Pollock   Three Planes   Forehead. Old Age.   Logan's Slogan

- He wanted to establish a travel company FAST FOOD which would transfer back to any time zone those rich believers who hadn't had enough time to eat well before fasting started.
- He wanted his own crossword puzzle magazine to have squares instead of titles, and that the titles changed every time depending on the answer to the question that followed.

- He wanted to establish an NGO 'Ouroboros',[9] which would get grants for only its own benefit.
- He wanted to make the entire population of the country millionaires and even elaborated the simplest scheme for that: if a million people sacrificed one euro every month, and all the raised amount went to one person, he would automatically become a millionaire; the second candidate would receive the same amount the following month, then the third one and so on. The only drawback of this scheme was that in this way only twelve new millionaires a year would appear in the country, whereas about three million nine hundred and seventeen thousand, four hundred and twenty-two people wouldn't be able to become millionaires while alive unless they won the lottery (which was obviously not invented for poor Matthew)...

...Finally, he decided to become a private detective. First, he looked for some cases, and next, he looked for the ways of investigating them. And since there was not a single veteran of the Afghanistan war living in his neighborhood, he himself had to describe the details of the crimes for the future generation. His very first case (*Disappearance of the TV Tower on the Mount Mtatsminda*[10]) turned out to be very cloudy, but while he was thinking about the possible ways of investigating this mysterious disappearance, the sky cleared, the clouds over the Mount vanished, and everything, including the Tower, fell

---

9 **OUROBOROS** – ∞
10 **Mount Mtatsminda** (translated as "Holy Mount") is in the centre of Tbilisi. The TV Broadcasting Tower is located on its top and can be seen from everywhere in the city, except from the Tower itself.

into place. This successful debut was followed by another equally successful one: this time Matthew had to find a *cat* instead of a *cat burglar* (*Dead or Alive*). True, the cat named Schrödinger returned home safe and sound without anybody's help, but nobody could deny the fact that Matthew had predicted its homecoming two hours earlier. Then there was a mysterious case of the naked man stuck between the window glass and the curtain in the building on the opposite side of the street (*The Ugly Truth*). But the neighbour's hubbie left so hastily that he didn't even try to raise the curtain to reveal the truth. So, Matthew, too, generously decided to leave this intimate deal unanswered, and described the details of the naked arse only in his annals.

Naturally, Matthew understood that for him all those series of investigations were only a kid's game played to kill time which he could not stop, but after several successfully investigated cases – *Lord of Fries* (much ado about nothing with the chef at McDonald's), *Swallowed Swallow-nests* (mystical disappearance of the soup ingredients from the local Chinese restaurant), *To Kill a Mockingbird* (conflict erupted due to chastising Schrödinger for killing a bird) – he assured himself of having brilliant skills for conducting investigations, and decided to switch to murders. It was at that point that he uttered his famous phrase: 'if Sherlock Holmes is in the WEST, then I am in the EAST!' and since merely imitating the famous detective seemed a very primitive move to him, he decided to become his opposite. So, he started smoking electronic cigarettes, playing the tam-tam, and employing inductive reasoning.

"There is no glass in the display case. The space for the

exhibit is empty. The area is surrounded with the yellow police tape... aha..." Matthew lowered his head, leaned his chin on an outstretched thumb of his left hand clenched into a fist, rested his nose and lips on his squeezed fingers and wondered whether the reader would have tried to copy his movements to better imagine his posture if he had been a fictional character. And after this brief lyrical digression, he easily came to an inductive conclusion: "It looks like a theft!"

"Yeah, yeah! Only thieves, rascals, and other lousy people visit this place, who else would?! You can't see here a single decent gentleman these days!" said the museum security officer waving his hands desperately. "Just a couple of kids are brought here on a school excursion and that's all!... for us the museums seem to exist only abroad – as soon as we go to a foreign country, we rush to the local museums – but here, in our home country, we hardly ever notice them; they are the last place we would like to visit! Of course, we are proud of our cultural heritage, so what? We still prefer to enjoy that of the others. Maybe it's because our treasure is here, close to us, and we hope to see it any time we wish. As for the Louvre, it seems somewhat far away."

"Or maybe because the Mona Lisa or Venus de Milo are not exhibited here," Matthew put forward his version and saddened a little realising that he could only recall those two exhibits from the huge collection of the Louvre.

"The Mona Lisa, you say, hah? But I've read on the internet that what they have on show at the Louvre is not the original painting painted by... umm... that man; the original is kept in a depository, they say, didn't you know that? So, what the visitors see at the Louvre is a copy, mere replacement, something like the stuntmen who fight instead of the main characters in Hollywood films. Even if the picture was the original, I would still hate the museums that are littered with all sorts of rubbish, you know… if you want to show the real things, you need to exhibit only a couple of paintings, not more. Otherwise, after loitering around the museum for ten minutes, the visitors don't care whose painting they see – Paul Gauguin's or Paul Gascoigne's.

"As regards the missing exhibit…" Matthew wanted to show his investigative skills.

"Oh, yes! And I adore the right to take one shot! Well, of course I have not been to many foreign museums, you see, but I judge by those I visited. Usually, it's not allowed to take pictures (so that others do not see the exhibits and all), but you can still take one picture! You click once and someone runs up shaking his warning finger at you as a way of showing disapproval, and you immediately answer: 'Excuse me, I didn't know; I won't do it again, mister!' But the picture – one memorable still from the whole museum – remains in your camera!… the main thing is to choose the worthy one!"

"What's lost?" Matthew was losing his temper and time at the same instance.

"The culture of visiting museums, the respect for our own culture, what else?"

"I mean the missing exhibit…"

"I also mean the exhibits…" the officer interrupted him again. "Earlier, for instance…"

…Actually, this was what had happened: in the State Silk Museum (a luxurious two-story redbrick building in the vicinity of a peaceful and cosy green park) a single silk slipper of our legendary Queen Tamar – the main and most valuable exhibit of the museum had disappeared. There were neither fingerprints nor any other evidence – nothing at all. Besides, the door and windows were locked from inside… in short, neither the police, and most importantly, nor the journalists could investigate anything. Even the security officer, who would more easily hold the thief than his tongue, was suspiciously silent about the incident itself. True, it wasn't the crime of Matthew's dreams (which would have been the case of murdering the security officer), but one could easily knit a silk cloak of grandeur from this case. That was why Matthew rushed straight to the museum as soon as he heard the TV news about this historical theft.

"The case is pretty complicated, Watson!" Matthew sighed deep in thought. But the case was quite simple; the complication was caused only by investigating it with the help of induction. On one hand, Matthew could hardly distinguish induction from deduction and was terribly afraid of using the method of that boastful Londoner quite by chance: on the other hand, investigating the case by induction was the same as to pour coffee onto sugar… or maybe not… anyway, as we have already admitted, Matthew could hardly distinguish induction from deduction.

"If I forgot about induction, I would easily conclude that poor attendance at the museum worries the security officer more than disappearance of the exhibit… in addition, historians describe Queen Tamar as barefoot rather than the opposite. But…" He paused, after which his mind should have brightened, "…it seems that in reality…"

"…There doesn't exist any slipper; it's all just a matter

of marketing, so that senseless popular fanaticism is of some use," a man who appeared in the hall from nowhere finished the phrase not even uttered by Matthew. The stranger had a short beard and short-cut hair, which could not be said about the guy painted on his T-shirt.

"Nonsense!" protested the security officer who was obviously offended. "I have been guarding that slipper for many years!"

"Of course, you have been guarding it, but *quis custodiet ipsos custodes?*[11] – that's the question!" the stranger answered in Latin to avoid tautology, and while the security officer (who had no way of reading the footnotes in this book) was deeply puzzled, he addressed Matthew: "It's high time you set about a more serious case."

"Only a murder case can be more serious for me!"

"That's exactly what I mean! But the thing is that the murder has not been committed yet…"

Matthew had no idea who this damned stranger was or how to investigate the murder that hadn't been committed; he didn't know which title to give to the previous case – *The Silk Road* or *The Silk Dead End*; neither did he know quotes by Socrates or who John Snow was, and under what conditions Chlamydomonas multiplied; he even had no idea what Chlamydomonas was or why he trusted the person about whom he knew nothing… nevertheless, he unconditionally agreed to investigate the case of the not yet committed murder, because against the background of so much ignorance, he

---

11 *Quis custodiet ipsos custodes?* **(Lat.)** – "Who will guard the guards themselves?" – This is the first and the last Latin phrase that you come across in this book. *Promitto* (Lat.) – I promise.

knew one thing for sure: you never need to refuse anything if your consent spoils nothing!

Spoiler # 3: Virginia Is Silvia's Sweetheart

"Why do we often fall in love with those who don't even like us? Or why do those we don't care for a wee bit fall in love with us?" Leah thought putting "Bestseller"[12] into her suitcase. And as nobody could give a reply to her thoughts, she went on thinking: "Maybe because the ideally balanced world is only a fairy tale reality, and the real life should be different in a way... yeah, the main essence of real life always lies in a constant struggle, while a peaceful fairy tale life, however fabulous, becomes monotonous and boring in the end... it's crazy to struggle for a little while in order to summarise the rest of your long life with a five-word fairy tale ending: *And lived happily ever after!*"

Leah never once had dreamed of being a princess. Moreover, the frog was only an ugly representative of tailless amphibians for her. Unfortunately, the one and only prince she would gladly meet lived on another planet code-named *B 612*. So, she distributed her life, which was not fabulous at all, according to several points among which she was fond of only four:

1. **Endless thinking** – Leah often thought that words in thoughts sounded much better than when uttered in

---

12 **Bestseller** – a title of the book belonging to the keyboard of the Author of this footnote.

statements. Swiftly editing them in her mind, she could create a masterpiece within the hour; take the floor and deliver an exciting speech in front of millions; win debates with the experts of using their knowledge of tangents and cotangents in their daily life, and even make up a brilliant dialogue for flirting. But as soon as she started pronouncing the words, they jumbled, deformed, and lacked some sounds; her phrases became overloaded with "er"-s, "umm"-s, "uh"-s, "like"-s, "you know"-s and the other filler sounds and words, whereas the important verbal structures just refused to roll off her tongue. She often compared her stubborn tongue with a swimming pool diving springboard created only for the most daring words. At times, when she started speaking terrible nonsense, it even looked like the pirate schooner plank which her words had to walk. On the other hand, she was able to *think* freely about anything in the world, for instance: why women in commercials always carried their favourite washing powders in their pockets; whether one's passion for the Latin language should be considered a case of necrophilia; how could the writers know what their characters were thinking about, etc.

2. **Fighting against clichés** – Leah tried to avoid all those trite similes like the plague. She also really hated the banal hyperboles, metaphors, and other figures of speech the names of which she often forgot like now. So, she was constantly looking for unique forms, which was a far more complicated task than to spell the name "Houellebecq" correctly at the first attempt, or resume reading the book,

abandoned several months earlier, without re-reading already read pages.

3. **The Animal Prince/Princess** – The cat was a bright and fluffy point in Leah's life. She adored everyone (from Halle Berry to Lloyd Weber) who had even the slightest contact with this animal. Because of such a love of cats, she even saw something positive in *cat*aclysms and *cat*astrophes. Little wonder she had a pet cat at home too, a pitch-black one, with a strange name – Eyed Peas.

4. **"More than a Rib"** – such was the name of the feminist organisation, whose strong and independent member Leah happened to be. Her main mission was to be very attentive and reveal the elements of sexism in everyday life. From time to time, they even organised small demonstrations protesting against everything, starting with the use of words '**her**o' and '**his**tory', that were sexist and *a priori* emphasised the gender differences, and ending up with the images of umbrellas on the doors of Ladies' rooms indicating that they could be used only by women. To tell the truth, Leah didn't understand the essence of feminism very well, but she knew for sure that there was a sea of information about the three waves of this trend on the internet, and despite the fact that she could not boast of any culinary successes either, she easily cooked one-pot meals for every man around.

"And yet, why do we often fall in love with those who don't even like us? Or why do those we don't care for a wee bit fall in love with us?" Leah wondered again, as if some unseen lazy hand transferred her initial wonder from the first line to paragraph seven with the help of the copying-and-pasting. She had never thought about such injustice until one character of the novel "Bestseller" (resembling Leah for not liking anyone or anything) made her think about it. She even wanted to address this question to the Author in a written form, but then found it awkward for two reasons: 1. He could have misunderstood her, thinking that it was just an excuse for starting a conversation, and 2. It would be ridiculous to say to the Author that she felt like being one of his characters. In the end, she decided to find the answer to this question herself, without the Author's help:

"If everyone liked everyone, love would fall in price, but God does not seem to be a socialist at all… wow!" Leah felt proud of her statement mainly for using the words 'God' and 'socialist' in one sentence. She was not too picky in personal relationships. The only prerequisite for her potential partner was **flawlessness**. In general, girls try…

"Why only girls?" Leah protested. "Doesn't it sound too sexist?!

…Okay, let's put it this way: in general, *people* try to find ideal partners when they themselves are far from ideal. So was Leah. Sometimes she didn't like someone's profile, and some other times she didn't like someone's profile picture; some young men wrote 'gonna', 'wanna', and 'gotta' instead of 'going to', 'want to', and 'got to' (those united contractions always reminded her of Frida Kahlo); some took her to MacDonald's on their first date (and treated her to the hamburger menu!); some preferred Van Damme to Van Gogh, and some didn't have the slightest idea who Kierkegaard[13] was (Leah didn't understand well the existential worries of that philosopher herself, but an ideal man should have known something about him, at least the right version of his name); some others used emojis more often than words, and still others couldn't use any words at all; for some X was associated with bookmakers rather than mathematics; some were tired of taking frequent selfies, while some others didn't mind taking photos, but instead of saying "cheese" stood with such a frozen air as if the Red Baron[14] was going to fly out of the camera… and Leah got tired of wasting the best years of her life looking for the ideal male. So, in the end, she decided that as love was blind, she could turn a blind eye to some trifles and stop worrying too much. And right at that crucial point, she saw *him*…

He was wearing a T-shirt with a photo of an untidy revolutionary with a very short name and very long hair. The stranger himself didn't look like a native guy – with pale complexion and refined cheekbones, he looked more like a west European visitor. "All men are identical… all men are identical… all men are identical," Leah repeated three-times, as if it was a mantra, but realised that if he had asked her, she would have gone hitch-hiking with him wherever he wished, even to the faraway galaxy, to stop the first and the only car that would be gliding around the planet to David Bowie's music.

---

13 **Kierkegaard** – Soren Aabye was a Danish philosopher and a lot more, which is not at all essential for our narrative.

14 **The Red Baron was going to fly out of the camera** – a metaphor used by the only boy who knew who Soren Kierkegaard was, and even explained to Leah that the Red Baron was the nickname of the best fighter pilot of the German Air Forces during World War I.

"I would gladly travel with you," the stranger suggested quite unexpectedly, as if reading Leah's thoughts…

why *as if*, though? He really read them as anyone else could if they opened this book to this very page. But the girl didn't know it yet, and ascribed this suggestion to the magic fluids that had appeared between them.  They got acquainted at the demonstration held in front of the café where the waiters were in the habit of giving the bill to the male diners, ignoring their female partners. When the demonstration was over, the stranger suggested checking it all in practice, and invited Leah to the same café in order to teach a good lesson to those potentially sexist waiters.

"I have always dreamed of travelling," Leah answered mechanically, but instantly added: "But I have no minute to call my own at present."

"Don't worry about time. You can lose anything but time during our journey."

Leah thought for a while. She didn't want to lose anything, be it time or her head.

"Suppose, I agree… where do we go from here?"

This question had a double meaning – it referred to both time and space.

"I'll tell you in the evening," the man said trying to sound mysterious, and then added: "Besides, the main charm of travelling is not where you are going but with whom you are travelling."

"Why me?"

Asking this question Leah hoped to hear: *because you are more perfect than the pearl in the earring of the Vermeer girl*, or *you are as interesting as the fact that nearly 3% of the ice sheet in Antarctica is penguin urine,* or maybe that *seven cats, one spider named Sleipnir,[15] and three children (among whom the firstborn would be either Lucy or Emile) would be running about in their future home...* but alas!

"It's a very significant expedition," whispered the man since he thought that whispering added an extra charm to any story. "In such cases, a woman's intellect and wit are very important"

"Well, well..." thought Leah, "doesn't it sound sexist?!" and was greatly disappointed. "Let him go to Hell! Without me!"

...A suitcase stood so majestically in the middle of the room, as if it was going to make the throne speech announcing his royal dreams to the co-suitcases. Three hours had passed since the promised evening started. The man assured her he would come soon, but the concept of "soon" with the natives ranged from two minutes to two hours. She gave him her detailed address in the café: the name of the street, the number of the building, which floor he should get to, and which flat he should look for (the iron door on the right side of the landing, with a Gigi Buffon sticker on it). The idea of purchasing a Gigi Buffon sticker belonged to Leah's friend – she attached it to the front door of Leah's new flat saying that Gigi would be her doorkeeper and would guarantee her safety better than the

---

15 **Sleipnir** – crossword clue: eight-legged horse ridden by Odin, 8 letters, the 5th letter is P.

image of the cross. And Leah liked it... I mean, she liked Gigi Buffon rather than the idea of keeping her flat safe, and every time she gave her address to someone, she proudly added: "the iron door, with a Gigi Buffon sticker on it."

"I should have figured out from the very start where we are going!" The level of Leah's anger grew as time went on. "I knew that all men are identical, but some prove to be even more identical!"

Leah's *identity theory of all men* soon collapsed (at least its anatomical basis staggered seriously) when there came a knock at the door, and after a few seconds, three completely different men entered the room. Sure, one of them was that sexist, non-punctual bastard; another was a tall middle-aged man with a short gray beard and obviously ill-fitted glasses on his nose, while the third one looked somewhat familiar to Leah, but... well, he had an easily forgettable-appearance of a person, whom you meet at someone's home party but can't recognise while travelling on the same bus a week later.

"Everything will become clear in the end," the sexist, non-punctual bastard (who turned out to be pretty rude as well) interrupted Leah's thoughts. So, Leah again had a feeling that he was reading her thoughts. "...The main thing is that all of us gathered at last, and since there are no other protagonists in the book, we can get down to business."

Leah was completely confused. She could not understand what the book had to do with all that... and even if it had, the fact that three of the four characters were men was clearly a gender imbalance.

"And yes... you needn't take any suitcases. In the location we're travelling to our clothes will be an anachronism anyway.

"Wouldn't you please explain at last what's going on? I've already lost several hours thanks to you!" the elderly man protested, and Leah guessed that 1. She was not the only one who rode the elephant in the mist, and 2. Constant search for original metaphors sometimes led to a disastrous end.

"If you tried to calculate how much time you waste on doing nothing, you would lose not only time but also the wish to calculate it," the young man with an easily forgettable appearance added, and looking at the faces of his addressees, decided not to say another word until his words would sound more important than his silence.

Leah put her suitcase at the wall and sat on a settee.

"You'd better all sit down now, because it'll take quite a while to explain everything," the sexist said stroking his beard with a strong hand. Then he clung to its end with the thumb and the index finger like a hero in a film clinging to the top of a cliff, and started telling his story:

"One fine morning I discovered that I was a fictional character and remembered only three things about myself..."

Literary Apocalypse

Spoiler # 4: Matthew will be Condemned to Death

23.04.2017 – It's pretty difficult to be a fictional character; all the more so when there are lots of cool-blooded Authors ready to write such terrible things as "deceased", "died", "was killed", "was stabbed" or "drowned", and their hand won't even flinch. Apparently, it's time for the world of literature to have its own Criminal Code, to sentence such Authors to appropriate punishment: "The court finds Gustave Flaubert guilty of causing Emma Bovary's suicide, and sentences him to ten years of writer's block. The verdict is final and not subject to appeal." Well, well... great, why not?! People are ready to protest against calling a simple unicellular organism the amoeba, as they consider it politically incorrect, but no one gives a damn about protecting the rights of characters!

30.11.2017 – After a long search, Becky Thatcher and Tom Sawyer answered our call from one of the caves. Thank God there were many strangers all around, and no one noticed my presence.

14.03.2018 – Too much time and too few books!

Memento Mori lived only *in the present moment* not because he was fond of the present, but because "future" and "past" lost all meaning to him. The thing was that his "tomorrow" might have arrived the previous day, his "yesterday" two days later, "the day after tomorrow" two days earlier, and "the day before yesterday" even after a century… in short, he was a time-traveller. Therefore, he never woke up where he spent the night, and never stayed until nightfall where he woke up. He decided to stay in Paris one single time, and there was such a massacre there that he could barely escape. After that night, Google became his faithful Sancho Panza, who was supposed to protect him from all potential ills.

04.04.1893 – I met Herbert Wells and told him about the time machine. He liked the idea and admitted that it was a brilliant plot. So, I achieved my goal – if he hadn't written his novel, I could never be able to move into it in order to steal the time machine, modify it, and travel in the past to suggest to him to write a book about a time machine.

"Time travel?!… (*Why do I always come across crazy people?* Leah wanted to think, but the phrase seemed too stereotypical to her.)… such things happen only in books and films, don't they?"

"Isn't it ridiculous when someone makes their fictional or film characters say that something happens only in books and films, thereby giving them the impression that they are real? Actually, you are all…"

Before Memento Mori could say that they were all fictional characters from a book, Professor Arno interrupted him: "Even if each sound you utter is true, we must clarify one thing before we proceed… as you know, the world is mostly ruled by two words: 'why?' and 'because'. Why? Because without curiosity there is no progress. But curiosity that is not satisfied loses all meaning. However, for the sake of progress, the question "why" must be correctly posed. For example, if Newton had asked *why did the apple fall on my head,* instead of asking *why did the apple fall,* we would get an existentially deterministic complaint, and not the law of gravity."

"Why have you started giving this lecture now?" asked Leah, and judging from the expression on the Professor's face realised that this was an inappropriate why-question.

"The reason is simple: before we start talking about time travel – the reality of which, despite my deep confidence in its possibility, so far seems impossible – someone should ask: 'why *us* out of seven billion people living on this planet?'"

"Why *us* out of seven billion people living on this planet?" Matthew inquired.

"Because, actually, we are…"

Actually, if Memento Mori hadn't have appeared in Matthew's life, his next case – "The Lady with the Cat" – would have led him to Leah, and after a month they would have conceived a child who, at the age of ten, would have concluded that Santa Claus is an old lumber sexual who exploits the Elves on non-working days and doesn't give a damn about protecting animal rights. At twelve, he would have dreamed about Sigmund Freud giving a pipe to Sherlock Holmes as a birthday present, not even recognising anyone or anything except the pipe. At eighteen, under the influence of Professor Arno, he would have been carried away by science, namely physics. At fifty he would have invented the most powerful explosive in the world, and at sixty-five, a huge supply of that substance would have exploded during an experiment in his laboratory and destroyed the entire planet – and so it goes!

28.10.1018 – I went two millennia back, caught a dozen butterflies and transferred them to our times. The only change that followed was ten more dead butterflies in our world.

Actually, the whole previous paragraph is a sheer lie. Nobody could predict how history would have changed if Leah and Matthew's child had been born, or if Hitler had been a vampire and fallen in love with Eva Green instead of Eva Braun; if the bullet had hit Jacqueline and not John F. Kennedy; if Giordano Bruno had lived on a flat earth; if the Aztecs hadn't believed in the stupid legend of the "divinity" of white people coming from the sea; if Columbus had taken along a better compass; if Barabbas hadn't committed a crime in those faraway days; if Adam and Eve had been more hungry and eaten the snake instead of the apple, and if I, instead of this long tirade, had written the following short sentence:

"Because, actually we are fictional characters!" Memento Mori finished his statement at last.

"Why?" Leah couldn't manage to ask the WH-question correctly this time either; in fact, she wanted to ask "How is that?"

"You've been born in someone's head, as simple as that! Someone decided to make you love thinking and cats or, to be more precise, to make you an activist who is fond of thinking about cats, so that the huge army of cat-lovers sympathised with you. Matthew was created to utter pseudo-wise phrases, and Professor Arno to seek ninety-five ways of getting into history… in fact, we are all the product of one mind, and live in one of the literary worlds out of millions. Each of us is bearing a part of the Author's knowledge and experience which he already has or will gain in the process of writing this book."

"And who is the Author?" Leah had always wanted to be a character, but at that moment she would rather believe in the legend of Nessie inhabiting Loch Ness than in what was going on.

"I have no idea. Probably some kind of self-opinionated blockhead who is currently typing this text and hopes that the abusive comments that he puts into my mouth will impress the reader and assure them of his modesty. He is a local God who can do anything in his world except for…

"Except for what?" Matthew inquired, though Memento Mori would say it even without any inquiries.

"…Except for submission of literary genres and trends… I'll try to explain it to you."

21.11.2018 – Before establishing who is the potential victim of the Author, I will have to protect all the characters in this book. For this, the best way is to travel in time. Along with time, the epoch, the genre and the literary trend will change as well, and the Author will be less likely to kill the character off. Naturally, he can come up with plague, vampires, tuberculosis, famine, or other more banal reasons, but I am sure he will not give up this literary game.

"If I got to the bottom of the matter correctly…" Professor Arno decided to tie all the threads of this obscene case into one conclusion, "…a fierce dragon cannot eat us in case we find ourselves in the era of socialist realism. And if we find ourselves in a fairy tale, we can give a Colt gun to Three Little Pigs so that they will manage to protect themselves from the Big Bad Wolf."

"Absolutely!" agreed Memento Mori, "But for this we must simultaneously remain in the era of postmodernism."

"Yeah, clear!" said Leah, but in fact too little was clear to her. Almost nothing. Nothing.

11.03.2018 – I was having some fig jam with rosemary tea for breakfast, and thinking about why people describe uninteresting and unimportant facts in their diaries… but I found no answer.

"And if we really are fictional characters, why do we bother to travel in time? We could simply find a refuge in a safer work of literature," Professor Arno looked through children's literature with his mind's eye, "for instance, we could go to Bullerby or Lönneberga."

"Because our goal is not only to save our lives; there is something more important than that, but I haven't mentioned it yet…"

20.11.2018 – My father died today… or maybe it was yesterday, I don't know. While time-travelling, the concepts "today" and "yesterday" become utterly relative. Father was a pseudo-scientist. Until his last day, he believed that some people from the future were sending special agents to give history its desired course. Among those agents were Jules Verne, Jesus Christ, Leonardo da Vinci, Gutenberg and even Zuckerberg ("two Bergs[16] – two peaks of the informative development of humankind!"). In the end, he even wanted to assure me of the reality of the apocalypse. On the other hand, I could not convince him that he was not a scientist, but only a simple secondary character mentioned in the book only once – namely in this paragraph – with such a common noun as "father".

"Our main goal is…

    Dan! Dada dan!

    …to save our planet…

    Dan! Dan! Da!

    …and the entire world from total extermination!

    Da daaan!"[17]

"The 666th version of Apocalypse… ain't you fed up with it?" bored reader must have thought. But we can do nothing – if you do not mention Apocalypse, some characters won't even make a slightest effort to be alive and kicking. Besides, when there are four of them, it's hard to resist the temptation of alluding to the four horsemen of the Apocalypse. Their vehicle will be a time machine and not horses, so what? Firstly, Bulgakov had already used the horses masterfully in the denouement of his novel, and secondly, we can assert that our time machine has 4HP engine, who is going to test it?

---

16 **Der Berg (Germ.)** – if you didn't know a single word of German, now you know it – "mountain". My congrats!

17 **Dan! Dada dan! Dan! Dan! Da! Da daaan!** – a worthless attempt to verbalise a piece of some sublime music (Hans Zimmer was too busy to give me a hand).

22.11.2018 – There appeared to be only three of them…
I must collect poor souls and hide them in some safer work of
literature… maybe I'd better take them to Robinson Crusoe's
Island or Thoreau's Woods.

…Robinson Crusoe's Island!!! Eww! It is absolutely clear that this event would make the novel uniquely boring. Robinson Crusoe, by the way, is not among the top ten books that one would like to have on a desert island. However, which of the books is worth having in such a case? To my mind, if one happens to find oneself on a desert island, the entire world literature from Homer to Margaret Atwood will be outweighed by a single book – **How to Build a Ship – a practical textbook for beginners**.

"What's the use of saving a fictional world?" Professor Arno asked sadly. All his conscious life, the poor thing believed that he was an unusual person, but now he found out that his entire conscious life occupied only two or three pages.

"But for us it is not fictional at all! If we get rid of the authoritarianism of the damned Author, then we can continue to live outside the book covers, and we will have a chance to get to another time and another story," explained Memento Mori, and Professor Arno firmly decided to postpone the end of the world at least until he finally came up with his final speech… however, he easily imagined the part of the body, which his audience would tell him to kiss in case the end of the world came.

The remotest past – A fellow stuck to me like glue at the
temple of Artemis. I had no money, so I gave him a lighter. He
could probably sell it for good money.

"In short," Memento Mori tried to summarise briefly all that was said, but realised that the phrase 'in short' only lengthened his statement, "since we agreed that we can agree on something, it's time to introduce my plan."

24.11.2018 – Events are evolving at the speed of light. Apparently, the Author realised that the evacuation of the characters created problems for the plot of his book, and therefore, helped me find my father's secret diary. A classic example of a commonplace plot, isn't it? Someone dies and digging in his things they find something that radically changes everything.

*The diary is thick and half of its yellow pages contain some formulas. According to my father's records, the Earth is an experimental project that is managed directly from the Earth itself. The coordinates of the scientists' workshops are kept in the strictest confidence, and for more security their locations **are scattered around five different places** in the literary world. What's most ridiculous, the coordinates of those places and how to find them are written on the last page of the diary. Well, well... our Author is either a complete amateur, or too insidious! So, it remains only to hope that I myself will not be the potential victim I'm trying to save... anyway, whatever you are, my good man, you should know that it would be the most predictable end that you can come up with. Yeah, yeah, you can believe me, I have travelled through many detective stories and I know it for sure.*

P.S. Judging by the diary, the mechanism which is called 'the doomsday button' in pop culture is also in the same territory, and if the experiment goes the wrong way, Baaang!

Apparently, someone has seen enough blockbusters, according to which I should be Bruce Almighty, but which of the two – Wayne or Willis – I don't know yet, because if I try to save the world, then the Author will kill some character, and saving the character will make no sense if the world is going to collapse.

So, we will have to save the world together!

Dan! Dada dan! Da da da daan!

"Doesn't it look like a trap? Ready coordinates, a hundred times exploited and already trite scheme of Apocalypse, the fate of the world depending on one person..." Matthew switched the method of induction in the case, "In addition, the Author can do anything he pleases with us."

"This is not quite the case," Memento Mori pressed his temples with the thumb and the index finger of his right hand; then moved the fingers towards each other passing over his closed eyes, gently squeezed the nose bridge from both sides and slid to his nostrils. "The character gains freedom from the Author as soon as the latter creates him. Moreover, he enslaves the Author and makes him submit and adapt to his individual traits and needs... can you imagine Sherlock Holmes, who takes windmills for giants, or Don Quixote, for whom an apple bitten off by Sancho Panza would be enough to guess that Dulcinea del Toboso does not exist? No way! The characters are like Pinocchio – they obey the Author until the moment he finishes creating them, but as soon as they come to life, they go their own way and force the Author to obey their desires."

23.11.2018 – Before getting to know the characters, I'll improve the time machine, as Herbert Walls's mechanism is very large and cannot go back in time. I will first visit the biography of Nikola Tesla and ask him to rebuild the device; then I will go through Heinlein's books and try to create the maximally minimalist design. It will take a lot of time, but that's all right, since the book has just begun and it is unlikely that anyone important will die so soon. My father has died and that's quite enough.

Visually, Memento Mori's time machine had more in common with time than with a machine. It was a little bigger than a watch and consisted of two screens – one displaying the dates and the other coordinates. He chose its design after the "novel-mobile", which he wore on the wrist of his right hand as it helped him to travel in books. It, too, had two screens – one indicating the Author, and the other the title of the novel.

"I believe you!" Leah said all of a sudden, sounding like a character in the detective stories published in yellow covers.

"And how can you speak our language?" Matthew had been concerned with this question since the very page he first met Memento Mori.

17.08.1985 – I took the universal linguistic apparatus from one of Vonnegut's opuses. It can translate anything from other languages into mine and vice versa. If God ever angers me, I will mass-produce it and sell it in Babylon.

"Ah," Memento Mori smiled and instantly realised that only "Ah" plus a smile would be a bit ambiguous as an answer. "In fact, we are all speaking our own languages, and "Mandarax" translates everything right on the spot. It's a special apparatus which I discovered in Vonnegut's book.

"You've stolen it, to be more precise!"

"Nope. It's not thievery; it's intertextuality."[18]

"What the heck is *intertaxuality*?" – Leah inquired.

"... *Textuality*, my dear," Memento Mori sighed for the first time. "It's nothing important. When Achilles speaks English in Troy, you are not surprised, so where did this linguistic scepticism come from? This is the era of postmodernism, after all!"

"You do not have to justify everything with post-modernism!" Professor Arno protested and thought that **Father, forgive them postmodernism, for they do not know what they are doing** might have been very impressive last words of his final speech.

While the Professor was thinking, Memento Mori inserted the first coordinates copied from the diary – latitude 51°30'29.7"N longitude 0°05'49.9"W + 01.11.1605 – in the corresponding graphs of the time machine, and as soon as he pressed the button everything messed up. The suitcase, the cat, the poster of Freddy Mercury, the chair and the little frightened mouse under it – all vanished without trace.

---

18 **Intertextuality** – an abstruse inkhorn term coined to stand for plagiarism – textual kinship with other works.

"What's _____?" Matthew was confused.

"The words _____," explained _____ Mori.

"What does 'the words_____?"

"The Author doesn't want _____ to explain, we _____ go, but soon _____ we can't _____."

"What can't we_____?"

"Take one another by_____, Memento _____ last energy. "Now count backwards from three_____."

"Three _____ one."

"Fuck postmod_____," _____ swore and everything illuminated.

Brief Survey of the Planet Kimkardash

"Imagine a solemnly decorated but invisible giant Christmas tree. It's space. Now imagine an ant on one of the Christmas toys. It's Everest – firstly, because of the coincidence in proportions, and secondly, because it's high time to stop comparing ants only with people." – *Doc. film "A Billion Metres above the Sky."*

"Humans are sceptics by nature. It is difficult for them to believe in the existence of miracles on a planet that has been rotating in solitude in an endless void for millions of years." – *Kimkardashian observation.*

Do not tell anyone what I'm going to tell you about, because no one will believe you anyway. I myself would not believe if anyone told me that we lived in a simulated world and our entire history was written in advance. Maybe this theory has already lost its relevance due to many films and books (or became outdated, like the conspiracy theory claiming that the Americans made the great mockup of the Moon instead of the great leap for mankind), but one cannot refrain from proclaiming the truth only because this truth has already been proclaimed more than once in different forms. Let us form the following hypothesis: **"Mankind is prone to self-destruction,**

and its history, no matter how it develops, will always end in complete collapse." Naturally, this consideration has the right to exist. However, for its refutation, the one-time destruction of the human race is not enough for at least two simple reasons: what if the catastrophe was pure coincidence? Maybe with an alternative development of history, everything would be different?

That's where Kimkardash – a small planet in the solar system inhabited by scientists – comes fully into play! Every Kimkardashian scientist hungers after finding such an ideal chain of development of historical events, in which mankind will reject self-destruction. Having found it, they will be able to introduce life to other planets of the solar system using their newly elaborated perfect template. To this end, Kimkardashian scientists re-create the Earth after each disaster, and taking into account the causes of the previous Apocalypse, introduce a new centuries-old development cycle (which according to the parameters of their planet, lasts for only six months). Along with this, in order to promote the alternative development of history, the Earth is frequented by ordinary Kimkardashians at key points in time. We know them as Gutenberg, Christ, Einstein, Fleming and so on. Kimkardashians are easy to recognise – they are often called "geniuses" and "divine beings". By the way, the uneven distribution of geniuses and common people on our planet can be explained not due to the fact that God bestows the talents on his chosen ones, but to the fact that most Kimkardashians visit the Earth for tourist purposes. However, there were several cases when they stayed here (they say that one Kimkardashian damsel even tried to become a trendsetter on the Earth, and truly succeeded in that!).

Kimkardashians look like people, since they created humans at their laboratory in their own image – in the image of Kimkardashians. The majority of males have a thin, long, turned up moustache, while females are keen on sciences. The experiment in which the Earth suffered from several destructions is conducted under their supervision. The first disaster took place when Kennedy was saved, the next one when Hitler was given the opportunity to win the war, still another happened when Zuckerberg was elected President, and one more was the aftermath of conquering Mars by Elon Musk, one of the outstanding Kimkardashians of all time. At this stage, the seventh phase of the experiment is in progress. In this version of history, Louis XIV is beheaded, Martin Luther King becomes the first person of colour to be the President of the United States, Rastafarianism proves to be the most popular religion, and the Japanese study the method of recording dreams in video format. In order to observe the experiment, Kimkardashians set up secret headquarters on the Earth. Just a few scientists have partial information about their whereabouts. The only Kimkardashian, who kept a diary and described in detail the whole process, disappeared one fine day, and neither he nor his recordings about the coordinates of the place can be found due to the lack of information. Some Kimkardashians believe that a local woman had a hand in that matter, while others claim that the case couldn't have ended only with 'having a hand', since (frankly speaking) 'that Earthling had more interesting anatomical properties'. What is most important, 'the doomsday button' is also kept in the same territory; Kimkardashians call it 'Pandora's remote control' and use it to renew the Earth when the situation on the planet gets out of control. This button can cause Noah's Flood, atomic explosion, glacial period, asteroid rain, loss of gravity, plague, Vladimir Putin, global warming, and even robot rebellion.

Here, of course, one legitimate question arises: If Kimkardashians are so advanced that they can already teleport, travel in time, have telekinesis, can walk on water, fly without an apparatus, change their appearance, conduct complex experiments, and do not even get annoyed when someone slurps while eating, how did they allow all the information about them to fall into the hands of a not very popular Author, who lives in a small country of a simulated world and dares to spread their secret? Good question, thanks! Although, when the Earth is threatened by the Apocalypse and it can be destroyed any minute, there is no time to respond to such intriguing observations. If you listen to people, they can even say that Kimkardash does not exist and that all this is bullshit… hmm! But we needn't trust sceptics. As one old Kimkardashian saying goes, 'never believe those who advise you what you should never believe!'

Travelling in Time and Genres

Rosencrantz and Guildenstern are in Another Play
(A three-act play)

Dramatis Personae:

Memento Mori – traveller in time and genres
Matthew – pseudo-detective
Arno – archeology professor
Leah – activist
William Shakespeare – playwright and poet
Miguel de Cervantes – novelist and playwright
Company – Shakespeare's Irish assistant
Mr. and Mrs. Martins – Mr. and Mrs. Martins
Spoiler and ***Spoiler***
Suspicious men
Witches
Passers-by
Lighting technicians
Rosencrantz and Guildenstern (who are in another play).

ACT 1
Scene 1
The Globe Theatre

(At the back of the stage, there is a platform where a play within a play, namely 'Macbeth', is performed. There is a rough sea of people around. Memento Mori, Leah, Arno, and Matthew are among the crowd.)

Memento Mori *(continues talking)*:....Our space is just a microcopy of the main world in which they write about us. But even if everything collapses here, the main world will remain untouched – there people will simply close the book and, completely sure that their tiny planet is not threatened by the Apocalypse (which seems odd enough to me), they will eat some ice-cream, or...

Leah *(suggests a better solution)*:...Criticise the Author that instead of such nonsenses he'd better write happy endings.

Memento Mori: Absolutely. So, before the Author shows his claws, we must put an end to it all. Otherwise, both we and this passer-by will cease to exist.

Passer-by *walks across the stage to the wings, having no idea of the risk he is running due to his sudden appearance in this last line.*

Professor Arno: Excuse me, but... should we speak in a more lofty style, using archaisms and metaphoric language of poetry in the era of Shakespeare? Or should the change of genres have no effect on our speech?

Memento Mori (*coughs and defiantly assumes the posture of a poet*): My Lord Professor, let me tell you /What's heavy on me, torturing my soul:/All's vain, methinks, do not you worry/The wicked Author shalt still put the words/He likes into your wretched mouth.

Professor Arno (*tries to play along with him*)*:* So be it! We cannot escape/The Fortune's will depicted in her books.

Matthew: Are we really in the 17th century now or is this all fictional like we are?

Memento Mori: This is the seventeenth century reproduced according to the knowledge of the Author; I mean if the Author is careless and he was too lazy to look for information about the seventeenth century, lapses are not excluded. For example, we might be standing in front of the stage because he thinks that there were no seats at all in the Globe Theatre. However, since he took the liberty of writing the book, he's probably not so stupid as to believe in the existence of witches and werewolves in this era, and we probably won't be in danger in that respect (*notices three witches walking on stage*). Umm... at least standing among the groundlings... (*while the performance continues, two men join the audience*)

The 1st Man: Today, we'll know the verdict of the rebels; this play was wrighted for that very purpose.

The 2nd Man: I expect the verdict that will be for the good of the people, my good man, you know. The snake shalt be well slain while 'tis in nest.

The 1st Suspicious Man: No doubt, methinks 'tis clear – if you have a chance to checkmate the king, then do it.

The 2nd Suspicious Man: Hush, be aware and say none! I'd also like to shed their dirty blood, but mind the walls that have ten thousand ears!

The 1st More Suspicious Man: None seemeth so much dangerous to me as warning 'Be aware' said in whisper.

Leah (*pushing Memento Mori with her elbow*): Do you hear them? Why do they use such a suspicious poetic narrative in public?

Memento Mori: In fact, this is their secret language, which we understand thanks to Mandarax. And it sounds so poetic due to "Shakespeare Mode" switched on in the apparatus.

Leah (*ignoring the wonders of technology*): are they planning some serious plot?

Memento Mori: Nothing much, just a little explosion in Parliament.

Leah (*astonished*): Aren't you going to prevent it somehow? If I were you…

Memento Mori (*interrupts her*):…I would read the history books once more.[19]

Professor Arno: Actually, the only thing we learn from history is that we learn nothing from history.

Memento Mori: I have already heard this phrase somewhere, while travelling in books.

---

19 In this ironical comment, Memento Mori alludes to an episode in British history when the Gunpowder Plot was planned in the House of Lords to assassinate the king, but it failed without Memento Mori's help.

Professor Arno (*not giving up*): The frequent repetition of history is a good proof of this.

(*On the platform, Lady Macbeth kills the king*)

The 1st Utterly Suspicious Man: At last, thank goodness! Even if it costs us dearly, I still want to witness fireworks clearly!

The 2nd Utterly Suspicious Man: Be careful, Guido, watch your wretched back! One might think your head is hollow but it still doth feel as burden for your neck![20]

(*They tiptoe off the stage*)

Professor Arno: We'd better make some plan, or else what was the use of going through four centuries just to watch "Macbeth"?

Memento Mori: We needn't make any plans. I think Shakespeare himself is one of the Kimkardashians. So, he must know the first part of the coordinate best. The main thing for us is to get into the backstage area.

Leah: What does Kim Kardashian have to do with all this?

Memento Mori: It's a long story, we drove past it a few pages ago… I'll tell you everything when it comes to other characters, not until then; the potential reader is unlikely to enjoy reading the same thing twice, I'm afraid.

Professor Arno (*returns to the topic*): Do you really think that Shakespeare will open his heart to the first person he meets? The more so to the first four people he meets?

Memento Mori: When he listens to one of my theories, he will have to.

---

20 The first night show of Macbeth actually took place in November 1605. As for 1606 depicted in historical sources, it was at the urgent request of Shakespeare ("Whims of the Famous Kimkardashians", Vincent Degas, *Kimkardash Publishers*, p. 106).

Matthew: Maybe it's better to reveal your theory to us first?

Memento Mori: Don't even try to reduce suspense and intrigue of the next scene by spoilers.

Matthew: Then let's move into the next scene.

Memento Mori: It's not up to me to decide.

Matthew: To whom, if not to you?

Scene 2

(The backstage area of the Globe. Shakespeare and Company. Shakespeare is sitting at the table. He sculpts skulls from the wax of melted candles. A gun and several posters hang on the wall, but I cannot clearly read by candlelight the inscriptions on the posters)

Company: Outside are people dressed in strange attire. They want to meet you, Master Will.

Shakespeare: Today I am tired, and so much so that I cannot come up with a worthy metaphor describing my state.

Company: They're not going to leave until they see you. As they said, they have to tell you something about the Parliament.

Shakespeare *(a little bewildered)*: Let them come in.

Company: As you like it.

Scene 3

(Shakespeare paces nervously back and forth in the wings. Enter Memento Mori, Professor Arno, Matthew, and Leah... but why is Leah mentioned at the end? Because she is

a woman? To emphasise the dominance of patriarchy? What sexism!... enter Leah, Memento Mori, Professor Arno and Matthew... that's better!)

Shakespeare *(tries to hide his excitement)*: What's the matter? What's happening?

Memento Mori *(insolently)*: Buenos Dias, Miguel!

Shakespeare *(even more confused)*: Call me William.

Memento Mori: Don't be afraid, we're from the future and no one will know it unless...

Shakespeare *(interrupts him sadly)*: Well, that is, in the future they will still find out, right?

Professor Arno: What?

Memento Mori *(with pride of Sherlock Holmes)*: That in reality Shakespeare does not exist, or vice versa – Cervantes does not exist.

Shakespeare: Yes, yes, you are right! There is no point in pretending that I am from the seventeenth century. When you are thrown into this era from the developed Kimkardash, you will go crazy if you don't find something to have fun with. In addition, I accidentally took a teleportation device with me... or maybe not quite accidentally... anyway, I decided that it would not be bad to dispel boredom. In this era, it is so easy to live in two countries at the same time without anyone suspecting anything. There is no television, no photography here, you see. If you get tired of toing and froing, in Spain you will say that you were captured during the collision and kept in dungeon for several years, and in Britain you will explain your absence by travelling with itinerant actors. Even if some drawings of the epoch are preserved, their authenticity and veracity will be difficult to prove. In short, you create fame for yourself in both countries, become two geniuses of the same era and your ego is happy... the only problem is that you cannot die twice. Therefore, I will have to make one of the deaths ambiguous... or Shakespeare and Cervantes will have to die on the same day.[21]

Memento Mori: Great plan. But we're here because of the coordinate.

Shakespeare *(used to the role of Shakespeare, continues in Shakespeare mode)*: I see. But I can't do it. 'Tis beyond my meekest power, My Lord. I asked my dearest friend, good Guido, to protect it as an apple of his eye.

Memento Mori: And so?

Shakespeare: He said the hiding-place is quite secure. A lonely tree stands at the edge of the country road, and is guarded by two very worthy men who never take their eyes off it.

Matthew: We are not interested in the safety of the coordinate, but in the coordinate itself.

Shakespeare: Wait a minute! Didn't THEY send you?

Leah: I am a strong and independent woman! I won't let anyone control me!

Shakespeare: Damn, damn! *(closes his eyes and shakes*

---

21 The claim that Shakespeare and Cervantes died on the same day is unreliable, although both died on April 23rd. The thing is that William Miguel de Shakespeare-Cervantes made good use of the fact that Spain was using the Gregorian version of the calendar and his death officially took place on April 23 first in Spain (he buried a completely different person so skillfully that the fake was discovered only centuries later), and then, on April 23 British time (i.e ten days later) poisoned himself with a potent poison in Britain. ("Kimkardash and Earth – "Connections, Secrets and History", vol. 5, p. 88.)

his head from side to side with an expression of regret) O, woe is me to hear what I hear! Sorry, but I can't let you go and stay alive. Company!!!

Scene 4
(The same, and Company)

Company *(rushes in)*: I heard ado!

Shakespeare: Nothing much, a tempest in a teacup. Make the gun thine friend and send these four to Hades!

Company: O, what divine lines! But this time, please, tell me so that I can understand you.

Shakespeare *(angrily)*: Take the gun and kill them, idiot!

Company: But shouldn't the gun hanging on the wall go off in the last act?

Shakespeare: If you kill them, that will be the last act! O, my God! What have I done to deserve this?

(Company obediently heads for the gun)

Memento Mori: Wait a minute... *(company freezes)* not you, you can go on... *(company goes on)*. This scene is already moving into complete absurdity. Either the Author has no idea about the years of Chekhov's life, or this is not even the seventeenth century at all, but simply a fiction.

Professor Arno: When you are killed, it makes no difference which century it is! What an archaeologist dies in me!

Matthew: And a plagiarist!

(Company takes the gun off the wall)

Memento Mori: Apparently, we're just in someone's play, where Shakespeare is also a character and not a historical figure. Accordingly, we can take refuge in another play *(quickly enters data in the novel-mobile)*. Get ready!

Shakespeare: Fire!!! *(flowers pour from the muzzle of a weapon with the speed of a bullet)*

Memento Mori: No time to count to three, we have to go straight ahead.

Matthew: If you managed to say this long sentence, and in addition, I also say something… well, I don't know, really…

(They take each other by the hand and disappear)

ACT 2
Scene 1

(Avant-garde English interior. In the middle of the room there is a luxurious wooden table made by a poor carpenter out of the trees cut down in Sherwood Forest. In the centre of the table there is an aquarium. Four medium-sized fish are swimming in it, whereas its bottom is covered with pieces of peeled potatoes. On the wall there is a photo montage – Little John on the background of Big Ben. Near the table there stands a bust of a bald Maria Callas. It is dinner time, so Mr. and Mrs. Martin are sitting at the table.)

Mr. Martin: I just can't understand why there are not completely meaningless dialogues in plays.

(Mrs. Martin lowers the spoon into the aquarium, takes out the water, blows on the spoon and tastes its contents sipping loudly.)

Mr. Martin *(proceeds)*: It seems very false when the

narration turns to the characters just when they are saying something very clever… I mean, if the play is really a reflection of life, it should be full of meaningless conversations, empty words, everyday trifles and strong language.

Mrs. Martin *(not paying attention to his worries)*: How is your cousin John?

Mr. Martin: John? Well, John is all right. Three years ago, he gave birth to a child.

Mrs. Martin: Oh, what great news! Did he have an easy labour?

Mr. Martin: I wouldn't say it was easy, the whole staff was against it – how can a man give birth to a child, they complained. But he is so stubborn, you know, if he decides to do something, no one can convince him not to.

Mrs. Martin: Yes, you are right. As far as I remember, giving birth to seven previous children, he encountered the same pretentious doctors… *(pause)* by the way, darling, it's time for us to think about a child too!

Mr. Martin *(bewildered)*: Now? Right here? In front of so many people?

Mrs. Martin: Yes, why not?

Mr. Martin: Okay.

(They close their eyes and start thinking.)

Mrs. Martin: Although, until we have a lot of money, it's pointless to think.

Mr. Martin: Money doesn't buy happiness, dear. Happiness is a momentary feeling of joy… say, when you win several millions on the lottery!

(Suddenly, a knock on the door.)

Mrs. Martin: Who's there?

Memento Mori: Etgar Keret.[22] *(he is the only one to laugh at his own witty answer)*

Mr. Martin: Etgar Keret who? Nah, it didn't work... Let's start the game at the beginning. Knock again, please.

(This time it's Matthew who knocks.)

Mr. Martin: Who's there?

Professor Arno: Mat.

Mrs. Martin: Mat who?

Matthew: Exactly. I was named after my grandpa.

Memento Mori *(bored with meaningless verbal diarrhea)*: A murderer is after us, so would you please let us in?

Mr. Martin: Okay, but let's play "Sphinx" first: if you solve the riddle, we'll let you in.

Mrs. Martin: I adore playing Sphinx!

Mr. Martin: Do you know how to make up with a woman who turned her back on you?

Matthew *(without hesitation)*: You should praise her back!

Voice from behind the door: Isn't that sexism?

Mrs. Martin *(sick of standing at the door, she opens it)*: What a coincidence. We were just talking about you.

Memento Mori: But we're still strangers.

Mrs. Martin *(offers her hand)*: Mrs. Martin.

Memento Mori *(shakes her hand)*: Memento Mori.

Mrs. Martin: Nice to meet you! We were just talking about you.

Leah: Let's continue our conversation inside. A crazy armed guy will be here in no time!

---

22 Etgar Keret – a Jewish writer, the Author of the story "Suddenly, a Knock on the Door"

Mrs. Martin: Come in, please! Anyway, I don't feel like wiping up the blood on the stairs.

(They enter the room. Mrs. Martin closes the door and sits down in an armchair.)

Mrs. Martin: Take a seat, please.

(There are only two armchairs in the room. Mr. Martin is sitting in one of them, whereas Mrs. Martin occupies the other.)

Memento Mori: We will be standing, especially since we squeezed into your play without asking permission. We will just solve one riddle and leave you.

Mr. Martin: What a pity! People can never live without each other, but they always think about parting.

Mrs. Martin: What a wise man you are, my dear! You probably also know why the god who created the world in six days is still too lazy to shave off his beard?

(Mr. Martin ponders his wife's question.)

Matthew *(proudly)*: Riddles are my forte. So, what are we looking for?

Memento Mori: A lonely tree standing at the edge of the country road, to which a certain Guido assigned two guards.

Matthew: Umm... however, I'm pretty good in some other spheres too.

Professor Arno: Maybe Shakespeare meant the very Guido Fawkes, who will soon be arrested and sentenced to death for trying to blow up the Parliament.

Memento Mori: And since he's the only one who's had contact with the guards, they'll never get to know about it.

Professor Arno: I think I got what you mean... but despite the similarity, "Guido" is still a different name, isn't it?

Memento Mori: You don't seem to have much contact with the British. When we rescued Captain Grant, he got very drunk that night and talked to me for a long time. I didn't have Mandarax then, and the only thing I understood from his speeches was the phrase "Do you understand me?" because he repeated it after every third sentence.

Professor Arno: We must have a try. The fact is that everything else matches.

(Another knock on the door.)

Mr. Martin: Who's there?

Company: It's Company.

Mr. Martin: Company who? *(pause)* Damn it! Today, people with strange names have been knocking on our doors pretty often!

Mrs. Martin: Have you got a gun?

Company: Yes, a huge one!

Mrs. Martin: We also have one, so we don't need it, offer it to someone else.

Mr. Martin: Wait a minute, he might be useful for our game. Let him answer why George Seurat, the father of pointillism, never got married.

Mrs. Martin: Say why George Seurat, the father of pointillism, never got married.

Company: Maybe because he never fell in love with anyone.

Mr. Martin *(irritated)*: You'd better find a more banal answer, thickhead, for instance: 'his only love married another man'!... remember, once and for all: though George Seurat was the father of pointillism, he couldn't easily get to the *point* of making a marriage proposal!

Company: Open the door and I'll remember it better.

Mr. Martin: And can you say why Van Gogh cut off his ear?

Mrs. Martin: And can you say why Van...

Company: Would you please stop repeating every word? How do I know? It was he who did it, not me... maybe he cut it off because it hurt.

Mr. Martin *(ironically)*: And Louis XVI was beheaded because he had suffered from severe headaches, hah?

Company *(intrigued)*: Why then?

Mrs. Martin *(coquettishly)*: He wanted to keep an ear to the ground, that's why!

Mr. Martin: I have always trusted you, darling!

Mrs. Martin: Really? But I didn't notice it when I told you that the naked man in my room was just a model.

Mr. Martin: I'm so sorry, I simply didn't notice the watercolours lying there, my most faithful!

Matthew: It's becoming too complicated, Watson! Time to leave!

Mr. Martin: Do, please! I'm tired of talking to this girl.

Leah: I haven't uttered a single word for the last five minutes, damned sexist!

Mr. Martin: For four minutes and thirty-three seconds, to be more precise.

Leah *(not giving up)*: You priggish sexist!

(They vanish)

Company: Wouldn't you let me in at least now!

Mrs. Martin: Come in, the door is open.

Company *(enters)*: Where have they gone?

Mr. and Mrs. Martin *(together)*: And where do the

ducks go when the lagoon in New York's Central Park gets all icy and frozen over?

Company: And really, where do the ducks go when the lagoon in New York's Central Park gets all icy and frozen over?

Mr. and Mrs. Martin *(pointing in opposite directions with their little fingers)*: There!

Company: Thank you for your help! Unfortunately, I was ordered not to leave witnesses anywhere.

Mrs Martin: Great. Anyway, we have no room for witnesses – we live squashed into this small room, which *(points to the auditorium)* does not even have the fourth wall.

(Company aims his gun at Mr. Martin.)

Mr. Martin: Spare me, please! Don't shoot; I have to finish writing "Game of Thrones".

Company: Did you spare anyone? *(shoots, water pours out of the gun, Mr. Martin leans back in slow motion and the jet hits a Sean Bean poster hanging on the wall)*

Mrs. Martin: Haha! Hihi! Hehe! Hoho! Huhu! Hbhb! Hjhj! Haha! Hhhh!

Company *(grunting)*: Damn it! Apparently, this is not the last act. *(disappears in the same direction where Leah, Professor Arno, Memento Mori and Matthew disappeared)*

Mr. Martin: What a pity! I hope he had a better aim in life... I just cannot understand why books devote so much space to absurd episodes.

Mrs. Martin: Because books reflect real life.

Mr. Martin: You're a real genius, darling! I would love to enjoy thinking about having children together with you!

Mrs. Martin: We'd better wait for the curtain to go down.

(Curtain.)

ACT 3

(A country road. A tree. Estragon tries in vain to pick up the feather on which he is standing. Vladimir looks at the road and, in order to drown out the gurgling in his stomach, holds his breath from time to time.)

Vladimir: I decided to get out of the habit of postponing things for the next day from tomorrow.

Estragon *(continues his efforts)*: It's all absurd anyway.

Vladimir: Stop it. You don't even know what absurdity is.

Estragon: I know very well. For example, it is absurd to create such an insurance company that will only insure the lives of butterflies.

Vladimir: And yet you are mistaken. In fact, every person has a destiny.

Estragon: And what is our destiny?

Vladimir: To do nothing.

Estragon: Magnificent purpose. I would do anything to do nothing.

Vladimir: Most people's destiny is just that, but they don't want to admit it.

Estragon: And what is it like to do something?

Vladimir *(shrugs sadly)*: If only I knew…

Estragon *(hopefully)*: Maybe Godot knows?

Vladimir: Godot probably knows. He is omniscient and omnipotent.

Estragon: How can you say anything about someone you've never seen?

Vladimir: Have you ever seen God?

Estragon: Is God omnipotent?

Vladimir: In any case, he was able to make most people believe in him.

Estragon: Most does not mean truthfulness. Most people plead with God to grant the kingdom of heaven to children burned in a fire, instead of asking why a merciful God allowed them to burn.

Vladimir: All this is absurd!

(With these words, four people appear on the stage.)

Memento Mori: Hello!

Estragon *(completely taken aback)*: Is it Godot himself?

Memento Mori: Godot!

Vladimir: You came, after all.

Estragon: We've been waiting for you for an eternity!

Memento Mori: Got stuck in traffic.

Professor Arno: Many thanks to Henry Ford for his great contribution to preserving the image of the non-punctual part of humanity.

Vladimir: And what will happen now?

Estragon: Saint Thomas! Still can't believe it!

Memento Mori *(ignoring Estragon)*: We'll take a look at the number inscribed on the tree and leave. This chapter has already dragged on so long that some Authors would publish it as a separate book. And you can already return home, as your mission has been completed.

Vladimir: There is no home, only this tree and us.

Memento Mori: Then don't return.

(Memento Mori reaches for a tree. Vladimir and Estragon are extremely disappointed.)

Matthew: Excuse us. He came out a little abruptly, but the truth is that there is no use in waiting any longer. We, humans, spend most of our time waiting for something.

Vladimir: And what else is worth wasting time for?

Matthew: Emotions.

Estragon: And if the purpose of waiting is just emotion?

Professor Arno: "That made it worth the wait," might come in handy too.

Memento Mori *(finds the inscription on the tree – 17"0" – and turns around)*: It's time to leave.

Estragon: If you promise to come back, we'll be waiting for you again.

Memento Mori: No, what's the point of the second coming?

Professor Arno *(in a whisper)*: Leave them the only thing you can – hope. They are so used to waiting that they can't do anything else anyway.

Memento Mori: Putting an end to waiting is always better than endless waiting.

Matthew: Actually, I was to say that.

Memento Mori: I don't know who was to say what, but it's really time to leave *(enters the coordinates of the next point into the apparatus – latitude 9°08'28.1"S longitude 58°36'55.6"W + 09.01.1908)*. The endings of the plays in which Shakespeare had a hand are never safe. Therefore, we must get out of here before this sentence is fin…

(They disappear, and Company appears.)

Company: Have you seen four people?

Estragon: Is there even one person left in this cruel world?

Company: Would you please clarify.

Vladimir *(in apathy)*: Godot is dead.

Company: I see, they still eluded me. Nothing can be done… *(aiming the gun at Vladimir)*. Forgive me. I have no other choice; I have an order. I have to kill everyone in the last act.

Vladimir: So many happy minutes in one day is already too much *(a shot is heard. Vladimir falls)*.

Estragon: It's better to die for no reason than to live without a purpose *(another shot is heard. Estragon also falls)*.

Company: Why doesn't it end? *(pretty discouraged and frightened he repeats)* So, everyone, he said, that is…

(Tears fill his eyes. He raises the gun to his mouth. The stage darkens. The silence lasts for several seconds. The stage lights up again and we see the Company heading backstage. He freezes like a criminal caught at the scene of the crime. He again brings the gun to his mouth and the stage plunges into darkness again. A few seconds later, a shot is heard and someone falls down. The stage is illuminated very strangely – from the side. Against the background of poor lighting, three corpses are visible in the centre – Vladimir, Estragon, and a Lighting technician. The Company has managed to slip away, it seems).

(Curtain.)

Spoiler # 5: Leah Is Kidnapped by the Author

Once upon a time, there was a Kingdom of Nine Seas ruled by a wise, generous and merciful king. The sun shone there in winter and summer alike, and the trees bore Flanders chocolate all the year round. The only drawback was that the king did not have an heir. Physicians and scholars were invited from all round the world, but attempts by the queen to get pregnant were fruitless. The healers thought day and night and offered the queen various medications, but their minds turned out to be less sharp than the sword with which the king cut off the useless heads of those charlatans.

Time passed, and just when the sovereign lost all hope, a sage came from the Far East. In his opinion, the cause of barrenness was the Royal Curse, which would be lifted if the king shut himself up in a tower in the dark forest on the night of the full moon... the sage, for his part, would remain all the night with the queen and sing various incantations to her. Soon the queen got pregnant and the happy king gave the sage a lot of gold and silver, and sent him home with a retinue of security guards. But the whole company was still within the State of the Nine Seas when the robbers attacked it and left the sage without the treasure and his head. Hearing this, the queen fell ill and died shortly after giving birth to a baby. So, the king was left alone with his beautiful baby daughter, who had beautiful oriental eyes.

The years went by, and the princess grew up like any other child, and as she got older, she became even prettier. Princes, knights, commanders-in-chief and even frogs came to the palace from all over the world with marriage proposals, but the heart of the princess, unlike the palace gates, was tightly closed to them. As if this were not enough for the poor king, fortune sent him a more difficult test: the princess changed her mind about getting married and decided to fight for the infringed rights of women. The king could not imagine that in his state there were women with infringed rights. So, he thought that his daughter had gone crazy and sent to her chamber a new wave of healers. They listened attentively to the princess and came to the conclusion that the voice of women really needed to be heard. The king was afraid that the princess' illness was contagious, and until it all turned into an epidemic, he beheaded all the healers and locked the princess in a crystal tower. But this precaution didn't seem to him sufficient, so he, in the name of saving the entire state, issued an order to execute all the infected: "Off with the heads of those who are off their heads!" This order became even more draconian after the princess escaped from her imprisonment in the crystal tower...

***

Leah couldn't have dreamed of a better place. The first thing that caught her attention was a sleeping beauty poster that called on women to wake up.

Near the poster stood a girl of fabulous beauty. She was wearing a short-sleeve T-shirt with the inscription "Never call me your little princess!" She appealed to the passers-by to punish Bluebeard to the fullest extent in order to stop femicide.

"Let someone spin the top, please! It seems I'm in a dream," said Leah who was so perplexed that she couldn't even think how banal this metaphor sounded.

"Not in a dream, just in a fairy tale," admitted Memento

Mori, and to be on the safe side, looked at the horizon to make sure that they were 'Far Far Away' indeed. "But that doesn't make me happy at all, for there are more things in heaven and earth of the fairy tales than are dreamt of by Shakespearean characters."

Leah, Professor Arno, Matthew and Memento Mori stood at the edge of a Grove, namely in the place where the jurisdiction of the Kingdom of Nine Seas ended and the territory of the Kingdom of Nine Mountains began. And while Memento Mori was thinking about what was more unnatural – the use of the word "jurisdiction" in the world of fairy tales or thinking about it in the present situation, Matthew noticed an information stone set up at the crossroads.

A man weeping bitterly was sitting by the stone and filling the beret of one barrel capacity with tears.

"Why are you doing this?" asked Matthew, in whom predisposition to familiarity and the spirit of a detective woke up simultaneously.

"I saw many who set foot on these roads, but no one came

back from there. If you return, I will tell you everything," replied the man who was still sobbing.

"Where do these roads lead?"

"I have no idea. I've told you that I have never seen anyone coming back from there!" the man was indignant and sobbed more than ever.

"The coordinates can be on all three roads," Memento Mori announced and walked over to the stone, as he remembered that his main purpose was to save the characters. "I'll take the left road, let Matthew go straight, and Professor Arno to the right."

"And I?" Leah braced herself to say "That's sexist!"

"Umm… you stay here and do your bit for women's rights. The poor princess is fighting all alone."

Yes! Leah was ready to fight to the last cells of her leukocytes, erythrocytes and platelets! She was ready to bring feminist discourse into this masculine society! She was ready to stand up for principles instead of princes! She was ready… oh, wait a minute…

"If you meet Puss in Boots on your way, bring him with you, please!" she shouted after the pilgrims and continued to give voice to her heroism.

***

"The voice of a woman has always been muffled in fairy tales, always! And I'm sick of it! I'm tired of being a princess. What's good about that? Every day they lay a fabulous table for you, and then they watch you and say not to eat this and not to eat that! They warn me that I'll get fat and princes won't like me. I don't care who likes me and who doesn't! And I don't care about being a princess either. What's the good in it? Suddenly, some dragon, ogre or some other terrible creature will appear and my father will immediately start screaming: "I'll give my daughter as a wife to anyone who defeats the monster!" You are the king, the lord of such a large kingdom, damn it, you have everything! Promise some land or gold, but no! It's always me who has to get married! Thank God, these dragons gained a little strength and their heads don't fall like leaves. If it weren't for my dad's riddles, I'd have to sleep with half the kingdom. And if I dare to protest, I'll immediately be imprisoned in the tower. Then I'll have to sit there, on the twentieth floor, and wait until a ray of sunshine flashes through my window and some knight saves me… I will most likely die in the hands of that knight from vitamin D deficiency, and let him call me a 'Radiant Beauty' then! If I am in such an awful condition, can you imagine how other women suffer? Snow White is believed to have been saved by the dwarves – thank you, not half! She became a direct victim of trafficking! The poor thing has to wash for seven adult men, cook for them, clean up after them, take care of the whole household… can this be considered salvation? Or, take Little Red Riding Hood. There are only three women in the whole tale. Two of them are devoured by a wolf, and the third is so stupid as to let the child go alone into the forest full of wolves! And Sleeping Beauty? Her whole role is to grow up and fall asleep. Most importantly, for what purpose? Only for a kiss of some sweaty, filthy and disgusting prince, who is worn out from a thousand troubles on his way! Unless you put on your best clothes and crystal shoes, get into the carriage, and shave your legs properly, nobody will even pay attention to you... and then these standards of beauty! In what a deplorable state poor Rapunzel is because of them – even if she walks through the forest only once, all the microfauna with Latin names move into her hair! It's rare when some women stand out in fairy tales, and even then, they are only evil stepmothers who destroy the reputation of the entire female race. Are stepfathers apologists for kindness? I cannot believe it! If a woman is not evil, she deserves only one sentence – "Soon the queen got pregnant and gave the king a golden-haired daughter or son". Is she a queen or an incubator? It's good that men cannot give birth, otherwise poor women would not be honoured with even this one sentence... who is always helpless? Who needs to be saved? Always a woman! Who should kiss a frog? A woman! Who has to sleep the whole story? A woman! Who..."

"It's good that I asked her opinion about cats," thought Leah enjoying the princess' monologue.

***

"Go to the right and you will survive!" Professor Arno read the inscription on the stone aloud for self-encouragement. "I think I have found the easiest way to get into history, if an unhindered path can bring glory to a person."

A narrow path meandered up into the mountains, and over the mountains rose white smoke. Considering the smoke, one could think that there was either a village or the Vatican there. Since Professor Arnaud was firmly convinced, that despite its small size, there was never any room for the Vatican in fairy tales, he set out on the road leading to a potential village. He walked and walked and walked, crossing nine mountains and nine seas, and very pleased that at his age he could walk so far, decided to sit down and rest by the river. The weather was pleasant and he was besieged by an army of trees. The trees had chameleons instead of leaves, and they changed colour according to the season.

"For God's sake, **help!**" The Professor heard the voice of an invisible being. "Please, my throat is dry. **I'm thirsty for life**"…

Professor Arno got up and noticed that in the grass on the river bank something was beating convulsively. "Even if it's Gina Lollobrigida herself turned into a frog, I still won't kiss her," he decided, but suddenly sweet childhood memories rushed before his eyes and he guessed that for the prospect of being together with Gina Lollobrigida, he would even kiss a slug. But his zoological self-sacrifice was in vain – instead of a slug he saw a prettier specimen of fauna in the grass, namely a silverfish.

"How can I help you?" Arno asked the fish putting it in the palm of his hand.

"Well, guess how to help **a dying fish** thrown onto the bank of the river," said the fish and immediately realised it would be better not to waste time on this long and cynical tirade and just ask to be thrown into the water.

"Should I make three wishes?"

Professor Arno decided not to miss his luck. He didn't want to pass up the chance of kissing Gina Lollobrigida.

"Two wishes," said the fish. I'm a **silverfish**, not a goldfish."

"You're not in a position where you can haggle over

quantity." Arno wanted with all his heart to get into history and come up with the best final words, but he also could not refuse kissing Gina.

"If I die, even your two wishes **won't be granted**."

"There are many silverfish, but only one life."

"Damn you!" the fish gave up at once on hearing this primitive wisdom. "But **be quick**, please!

It's easy to say 'be quick'! Arno had been waiting for this unique moment all his life. He took a deep breath of air.

"I want to get into history."

"A very vague desire. Once an ogre caught a friend of mine and asked him for **exactly the same** thing.

"So?"

"Well, his wish was granted and he got into history as **the first ogre who was sentenced to death**.

Professor Arno thought for a moment. He could not rely only on the imagination of the fish.

"I'm suffocating, let me go, I beg you…" said the fish, and for greater certainty, stuck out its tongue.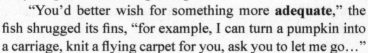

"Wait a minute! Then show me young Gina Lollobrigida right now."

"You'd better wish for something more **adequate**," the fish shrugged its fins, "for example, I can turn a pumpkin into a carriage, knit a flying carpet for you, ask you to let me go…"

"Damn it! All right, then come up with such final words that no one has ever said in the whole wide world," Arno tried not to miss the last chance.

"**Water**…" said the fish.

"Something better!" protested Arno, and a few seconds

later realised that this was the final word of the fish itself.

Thus, all the dreams of Professor Arno have sunk into the water along with their murderer. All of a sudden, two royal guards emerged from the ground.

"Did you kill the fish?" asked one of them.

"It died by itself."

"You ddd... didn't let it go, ddd... did you?" clarified the second.

"I was just about to, but..."

"Killing a fish, by order of the Gracious King, praise be to his name, is punished to the fullest extent, as well as sitting by the river, looking at the sky, talking with fish and arguing with us."

"Yes, but I'm not arguing with you."

"And what are you ddd... doing now, in your opinion?" asked the second ironically. "You mmm... must come with us."

"Where?"

"Our Gracious King, praise be to his name, thinks that curiosity often leads to trouble," said the first, "so, it is also punished to the fullest extent."

"CCC...Curiosity killed the Puss in BBB... Boots."

At first, Professor Arno decided to run away, but soon realised that one can't run away from one's age, especially after crossing nine mountains and seas. Therefore, he used all the remaining energy to get up, looked sadly at the smoke, the origin of which would remain a secret to him forever, and turned to the guards: "Let's go. But mind that I don't feel like losing time."

"Losing time is nothing compared to losing your head,"

the first one smiled and snapped his fingers. Suddenly, a carriage with bars appeared from somewhere and Professor Arno, with the courage of an innocent person, got into this unusual taxi in order to travel back down the path that he had walked. They drove and drove through nine mountains and seas until they reached a crossroads near the border.

"...And that's not all – women are killed one after another right at the beginning of fairy tales so that their husbands marry new ones! If death is a mandatory element for the development of the plot, let men die and women get married for the second time. But no! And what are these idle fairies doing, after all? They take tons of gold from other kingdoms, but don't want to do anything. They dressed up Cinderella for that accursed ball only once, and that's all they constantly write about in their reports..." Professor Arno heard a familiar voice. Then near that voice he noticed Leah. But before he could say anything, the guards whipped the horses and the carriage rushed towards Schrödinger.

"I hope I can think of some good final words before we get to the place of destination," thought the Professor, "At least something like: *life is too short to utter such long sentences.*"

***

"Love is like an appendix – you can easily live without it," Matthew reassured himself and for some reason thought about Leah. He didn't remember how he got to that, since the last thing he was thinking about was whether the biography of the famous Peter Pan begins with the stereotyped words *He was born and raised*, or his biographers are limited to the words *He was born*. It was not easy to find the logical link between Peter Pan and the appendix... anyway, Matthew now was walking along the path in a grove of singing trees and thought about Leah, or about love, or just about who we think about when we think about love.

"If you need some place to approach, you need to ride in a comfortable coach, tram-ta-ra-ram," the trees were singing merrily. And Matthew came up with an idea doomed to failure from the very beginning: singing trees in the city, to which you connect via the internet and indicate which music to play at a certain place on your route! In this case, you would have to invent such equipment that could decode one composition in different ways for different individuals... and then he guessed that such equipment already existed under the name earpiece. So, he changed his mind about turning these trees into a tourist attraction and simply decided to test their communication skills:

"Do you know what happens at the end of this trail?"

"It's full of goblins and trolls, tra-la-la, the eaters of souls, tra-la-la..."

The trees sang so cheerfully that Matthew was not at all afraid of the prospect of meeting those monsters. So, he sat in the shade under the elms, and decided to take a nap. A sweet sleep for him was something like the dessert of the day. As for falling asleep, it always took him as little time as covering distance between two eyelashes would. This time he had some very strange dreams: first he dreamed that young Keanu Reeves was bitten by a vampire: then he dreamed how Tim Burton made a biopic film about Johnny Depp, where the role of Johnny was performed by Juliet Binoche; and in the end, he dreamed about Robert De Niro asking Little Red Riding Hood for more money than was the standard fare for driving her to her grandmother's house by a shortcut. But he did not sleep long. First, he heard heavy footsteps, then an indistinct muttering, and in the end, still half asleep, he felt how the shadow of a huge creature fell on him.

"Thou who art there, ding-dong, should be in despair, ding-dong…"

Matthew opened one eye and closed it so quickly that his eyelashes ached. In front of him stood a terrible monster with many heads and an appearance much more terrible than described in fairy tales.

"Hello!" said the head on the extreme right side. "I hope you won't jump to your feet and run away screaming."

Matthew was about to do so, but when he imagined himself running with screams and the trees singing after him: *Look at this scaredy cat, ta-ra-ram, running away like a desert rat, ta-ra-ram* or something like that, he immediately changed his mind.

"Don't be afraid, we are wholehearted vegetarians, in body and soul," the fifth head of the monster reassured him, "they attribute so many bad things to us, including cannibalism."

"So, you are… umm… so, why do they cut off your heads?"

"The trouble is that there were a couple of carnivores in our family and their ugly behaviour was attributed to all of us. But I am… we are peaceful, we won't even step on an ant."

Matthew looked at the monster's foot and strongly doubted the correctness of the last statement.

"At one time, we were normal people living in the south

of the kingdom. But then the atomic tower exploded. One little BANG and everything went to hell! So, now we have nine, six and so on heads. Those who managed to leave in time, have only three... then the palace storytellers noticed us and came up with a thousand terrible tales about us. After that, everyone who can lift a sword wants us to be decapitated."

"What? What do they want?" The second head asked.

"Our decapitation," replied the third.

"What does it mean?" the fourth one was interested.

"Ah, he just wants to seem very smart-mouthed, you know, using those strange words!" the fifth snapped.

"In my opinion, this means beheading," the sixth expressed his modest opinion.

"Then it should have been said so, what's the point of showing-off," the seventh snorted.

"What's going on? What are they arguing about?" the ninth head asked the eighth.

"I don't know really; they might be discussing the matter of our beheading," suggested the eighth.

"So, that boy wants to behead us, does he?" the ninth got scared.

"God!" cried the seventh.

"What happened?" inquired the sixth.

"It turns out this boy wants to cut off our heads," explained the fifth.

"He must be a spy from the palace," the fourth concluded.

"We're retreating!" shouted the third.

"Please don't cut off our heads!" pleaded the second.

"Please!" added the first, "we are already an endangered species..."

"What did you say?" the second tried to clarify.

"Antiquated," answered the third.

"What does that mean?"

…Matthew silently listened to the conversation of the monster's heads for half an hour and came to the only conclusion: the first head was too developed in order to have eight more. Only the first head told him about the discrimination that the monsters were subjected to. They either cut off their heads, or sent serial killers to them under the code names of Siegfried and Beowulf, or simply intimidated them by making inscriptions on the walls of their houses: "Nine heads are good, but one is better!"

"It's all because of the storytellers. The king finances them and conjuncture…" the first head began, but immediately realised that it was better to choose a more understandable word, "…and they write what they are instructed."

"That's why in all fairy tales the kings are *wise, generous and merciful,*" confirmed the second.

"And the princesses are beautiful," added the third, "except the previous one, of course. You should have seen her! The poor prince, when he got drunk, kept saying that he kissed her only because he hoped that she would turn into a frog."

"Thank God Leah doesn't hear him," Matthew muttered, "otherwise she would think that eight heads were quite enough for this monster to exist."

"Come on, let's not blame only the storytellers," grumbled the fifth. "If we ever degenerate, it will be because of our complete ignorance."

"We shouldn't blame the system of education for every-thing," the second and eighth heads protested.

"When you can't tell the difference between a cobblestone and a young cheese,[23] it's lack of intelligence, not a problem of education, bro," confirmed the sixth.

Matthew had wanted to leave for a long time, but the verbal altercation between the monster's heads was so tight that he could not insert a word. "There has to be some way out, between the phrases *'you, stupid head'* and *'let's stop scolding one another, bros'*, uttered by the heads," he thought and yawned from boredom. Not even a second passed when the first head also began to yawn, and as yawning is contagious, the second, third, fourth, fifth, sixth, seventh, eighth and ninth started yawning too. Since it is not recommended to speak during a yawn, the heads fell silent. "It's time to say goodbye," said Matthew at last, and while the monster wiped a tear from eighteen eyes with his two hands, he added: "Take care of your heads."

"The right decision," said the first head, which was the first to stop the post-yawn procedures. "By the way, we woke you up just to advise the same. Ever since a state of emergency was declared in our kingdom, sleeping in the shade of a tree is considered a serious crime... if you had been discovered by the king's guards, they would have sent you to a dungeon at once."

"And there, you know..." The second head put its index finger to the left side of the neck and quickly moved it to the right.

"And please mind your head! If you happen to come into

---

23 In a famous Georgian folk tale, the protagonist convinces the monster that he is the strongest man in the world and can squeeze juice even from a cobblestone. Instead of a cobblestone, he squeezes the juice from a young cheese, and then... but that's another story.

contact with the king, agree to everything he says."

"Who has extra heads to argue with him?"

"First he will execute you, and then order his storytellers to write such terrible things about you that in the eyes of the people he will become a hero and not a murderer."

The nine mouths of the monster turned out to be yappers, so Matthew decided to round off with waving his hand without a twinge of conscience. Hardly had he walked eight hundred furlongs,[24] when a carriage with bars appeared behind him. Two men – royal guards – were sitting on goats, and two more were sitting in the barred carriage – the previously familiar nine-headed monster and Professor Arno!

Matthew tried the method of induction, but before he could come to some conclusion, the guards had already appeared before him.

"Have you walked eight hundred furlongs?" asked the first guard.

"Sorry?"

"Have you www... walked eighty hundred chchch... chains, that is three thousand and two hundred rrr... rods?" explained the second one.

"Sorry?" Matthew didn't change his expression.

The nine-headed monster tried to give some kind of sign, but when you have to logically connect nine different facial expressions with two different hand gestures, life becomes very complicated.

"By order of our Gracious King, praise be his name, walking eighteen furlongs is punished to the fullest extent, as well as standing on the road, listening to the singing trees

---

24 Furlong = 10 chains = 40 rods

at no cost, using the word 'sorry' when talking to us, raising eyebrows in surprise, and agreeing with all this without uttering a single word."

"I'm a detective!" Matthew tried to resist.

"Using foreign words is also punished," the voice of the first guard became somewhat harsh.

"By ddd… decapitation," the second clarified, and gave the monster an ironic look.

"Follow us and our Gracious King, praise be his name, will decide the rest himself."

"Let it be your way," Matthew sighed. "Lowering the curtain sometimes means intermission, not the end of a show. And one more thing I wanted to admit – by the law of the genre, one of you has to be "a good cop".

The carriage set off.

"No one will have mercy on you, du-be-do, enjoy the moment, don't be blue, du-ba-bi-do," the trees started to sing but Matthew could enjoy neither the moment nor their singing.

***

…One fine day, a new group of infected was brought to the palace: a nine-headed monster, an ageing killer and a boy who boasted of his strange profession. The merciful King did not want to keep them waiting for a long time and decided to behead everyone in the early morning… a bit later, a strange guest paid a visit to the palace and insisted on meeting with the misogynist King. The viziers fell into despair – no one knew what "misogynist" meant, and accordingly, they could not decide whether the guest should be punished for insulting the

King or rewarded for praising his majesty. While the viziers were conferring, the guest boldly entered the main hall and asked the King to release his friends in return for healing the princess. The King agreed on one condition – first, the guest had to guess his riddles. In case of refusal, he would also be beheaded for invading the palace. The King's guest said that his majesty was an "autocratic leader", which stunned the viziers once again. Although, since no one had guessed the riddles of the King until then, they decided that he would still get his due. The news of the riddles did not trouble the visitor; on the contrary, he asked to start without delay, since he and his friends did not have time to entertain themselves with children's entertainment. And so, the King began...

***

On his way to the palace, Memento Mori had to confront seemingly insurmountable difficulties. Sometimes he was just lucky – the Ogre, for instance, had a runny nose and couldn't smell a human on returning home; another time he calculated everything in advance and stocked up enough meat to feed the fantastic Firebird during the flight, so as not to have to cut a piece of his own thigh to feed it.[25] Elsewhere, he assured the Dragon that satisfying personal ambitions by cutting off drinking water for the population was one of the symptoms of an inferiority complex, and moreover, such behavior could become the Sword of Damocles for him, since in fairy tales, good usually triumphed over evil, and the

25 In Georgian folk tales Firebirds often help heroes by taking them to the place of destination if the heroes feed them the meat of their own thigh.

Dragon, regardless of its past, had always been stigmatised as evil by fairy tale standards.

Memento Mori also found out that the Raven sitting on a rock was saving his droppings to export them as fertiliser to foreign countries; and that the palace treasurer had sold the mortgaged house of the couple, who now slept on the axe blade; and that the man accused of killing his wives dyed his beard purple to hide from the King's guards; and that the headless horseman lost his head and hat while running away from a Dragon; and that the deer reached the sky with its antlers only because of a hormonal disorder.

However, part of the coordinate was nowhere to be seen. So, Memento Mori decided to go back, in order to at least refute the axiom "If you go to the left, you will die". On his way back he heard a secret conversation in a tavern: it turned out that one peasant had seen how the King's guards arrested a nine-headed monster along with a strangely dressed young man on the road to Schrödinger, and was worried that soon all over the kingdom... but Memento Mori had no time to listen to his predictions about the near future. Before saving the world, he had to save those heroes who were supposed to save the world. So, he went to the local second-hand market, bought boots with pretty plucked wings and flew to the palace...

..."The question consists of eight letters and the answer consists of six. What's the answer?"

By Memento Mori's rough calculation, this question consisted of many more letters, approximately fifteen, if the King... and suddenly some neuron in his brain finished the phrase in an instant... did not mean the word "answer" itself.

"Answer," replied Memento Mori.

"Wow!" the amazed King raised his left eyebrow three and a half centimetres, *"Ti seod ngihtyreve I od, s'tahw taht?"*

"Rorrim!" Memento Mori's eyes reflected the King's indignation.

"Hell!" The King banged his fist on the table, and had they not been in a fairy tale, he would have cursed at least using the word arse. "Well, let's see how you can handle this one: I have no legs but I can dance, touch me and I'll disappear at once. Believe me!"

"Snowflake," Memento Mori said so calmly and self-confidently, as not to create the illusion of confusion while guessing this difficult final riddle.

There was a deafening silence in the hall – the King was at a loss for the first time!

"What's the matter with you, Your Majesty? Cat got your tongue?" asked Memento Mori.

"Releeeease the detaineeees," mewed the King, "but firrrst, let himmm heal the princessss!

And Memento Mori did so...

"...Someday, I hope, the era of biased storytellers and jaded fairies will come to an end, and women will truly live fabulously," the princess smiled sadly and sighed deeply. "Forgive me, it seems my speech took too long."

Leah didn't even notice that the monologue had taken too long. The only discomfort was her swollen right leg, and she simply sat down by the edge of the wood to have a rest. The princess fascinated her so much that she did not even notice the arrival of Memento Mori and the royal guards.

"You must return to the palace, princess, there is no other way out," Memento Mori got straight to the point.

"There is no other way out," Leah teased him. "Cowards invented this phrase to justify their cowardice!"

"Let it be so, but her protest brings worse results – innocent fairy-tale creatures die just because they were born in this kingdom and think differently."

"Even if I return, the King will still continue to put people to death, he is like that, he exults in the death of others."

"Maybe, but in the future, it will be difficult for you to live with this responsibility. By staying at the palace, you can at least save some lives. The choice is yours: either myriad creatures will die because of you, or some of them will be saved thanks to you."

"Do not give up!" Leah frowned, "Don't take away the last hope of the women living in this kingdom!"

"O yes, of course! It will be much better to leave the children without their mothers who'll be executed; this is the best way out!" said Memento Mori, who hated to refer to children in his arguments, but could not think of anything better. "You need to fight from within, since waving your fist from afar is just populism. When you feel safe, self-sacrifice seems easy."

"I don't know," said the princess, "I need to think."

***

The King considered the cure of the princess a great miracle. The epidemic gradually subsided and then came to an end. Time passed and the prince from a distant land visited the kingdom of the Nine Seas. The King liked him very much and soon decided to marry the princess to him. The fabulous wedding feast lasted nine days and nine nights. Guests came from all over the kingdom. I was there too and had a good time. Since then, love and kindness have reigned everywhere.

***

"…You're a real scoundrel! all men are the same!" Leah wanted to wake up in herself Desdemona and Othello at the same time, and to reprimand herself for having agreed to accompany this conformist on his trip. "Now, palace storytellers are likely to write that the princess married an ideal prince and they will live happily ever after! Are you content?"

…Having gained nothing but disappointment, experienced fear, unbridled anger and current confusion, they were again sitting at the edge of the same grove from which they had begun. As for the part of the coordinate, no one, including the Author, knew what had happened to it.

"Maybe the numbers carved on the tree were just a coincidence, and the cat's tail is buried in a completely different place." Having been on the verge of death on the scaffold, Matthew decided never to be categorical and never to put his head on the block for anyone.

"I took you here to solve puzzles and not to turn yourself into a puzzle," said Memento Mori and suddenly realised that the notorious royal riddles had been chosen on purpose, and that the answers to them – *answer, mirror,* and *snowflake* – could have been the code of the main safe! "I have a version. I must visit one queen. Wait for me here, I'll be back in no time…"

…Memento Mori returned very soon indeed, holding a red apple in one hand and a piece of paper in the other.

"Stupid woman! How can she use the same method for everyone?" he grunted and crushed the poisoned apple with his foot. "At first, the mirror also did not want to answer, but when I said to him: *mirror, mirror, tell me, please, who is the angriest person in the world? Who is going to smash you to smithereens if you refuse to answer?* he decided he'd better bend than break and immediately said everything."

"A person's stupidity is not determined by gender!" Leah was reluctant to listen to Memento Mori's boast. All her initial faith in him was breaking down before her eyes.

"Let's discuss this topic later, as now it's time to say: *they lived happily ever after*," Memento Mori cut her short, and was just about to enter new coordinates (latitude 42°16' 2.6"N and longitude 42°43'09.8"E +1326 B.C.) into his machine, when Matthew stopped him – he did not want to leave without revealing the secret of the sobbing man.

"We're back, you see," said Matthew gloatingly to the crybaby. "So, tell us why you're crying."

"I'm such a minor character that even in postmodern literature I can't be someone's allusion," the man expressed his pain.

"Why are you gathering your tears in a one-barrel beret?"

"I want passers-by to ask me why I'm crying," he answered and burst into tears once more .

Matthew did not really understand anything, so only advised him: "Crying is not bad, but beware of dehydration." And while the man managed to blink his eyes to squeeze out more tears, Matthew disappeared from the fairy tale in the blink of an eye.

Spoiler # 6: Dies in the End

"It's a trap!" Memento Mori looked at the child whose eyes were filled with tears. "Literary trap."

In fact, he didn't expect it to end as easily as it began. None of the sane Authors would let the characters find something, which they were supposed to find at the end, at the beginning of a chapter; it would be the same as to give Ostap Bender a chance  of finding the treasure in the third chair, and make him look for the rest of the chairs just for the purpose of completing the collection. However, the letters, that were supposed to fill out the main coordinate, were written exactly where the travellers ended up. So, this would have been the shortest chapter in the history of short chapters if the time machine and novel-mobile had not simultaneously refused to act. Memento Mori understood the reason for this later – they apparently had ended up in an interlude inserted in the main narrative, and in order to continue the journey, they had to return to the frame of the main story...

"What does it mean?" asked Matthew.

"Well, how to explain it..." Memento Mori knew pretty well how to explain it, but he chose a complicated way, like someone who starts a sentence with the words "I don't know how to say this", and then continues to talk for quite a while. "For example, the world in which Scheherazade invents fairy tales is the frame story, the main part of the action, and what she tells Shah, that is, everything that happens in her folk tales, takes place in another world of, so-called, nested stories, since their plot develops in a different time and space. If in these nested stories someone tells something that happens again in a different time-spatial reality, we'll get one more embedded narrative... I guess I don't explain it very clearly, do I?"

"It turns out that this is all like what happens in the film with DiCaprio."

"Yes, something like that – the dream that you see in a dream, which you see in a dream, which you see in a dream. But it's transferred to the literary space."

"And what should we do?"

"Actually, in order to return to the frame of the main story, we need to reach the climaxes in the nested stories. The climaxes will be followed by the denouements, and the embedded narratives will come to an end, automatically raising us one layer higher."

"But it's the Authors who reach the climaxes in their stories, not the characters."

"No no, the Authors are forced to activate the characters, taking into account the personal qualities that they themselves impose on them. Otherwise, involving a character without a function in a narrative will indicate the weakness of the Author. This is what I would call our advantage.

**

A warm spring breeze gently swayed the newly blossomed foliage of trees in the orchard.

It is impossible to imagine a worse beginning of a story! Even such initial sentences as: *When it rains, my windows silently cry*, or: *The warm urine of a chameleon thoroughly soaked the desert sand,* are much better. But what can be done if a warm breeze really sways the newly blossomed foliage of trees in the orchard? As for the perfect functioning of the kidneys of a chameleon, we'd better not go into further details about it. From the depths of the garden came the children's hubbub. The gardeners were working silently. A man was sitting in the shade of the trees and watching the children play, but it was clear that his thoughts had carried him far away – somewhere to his childhood, at the time when the tree seemed to him a ladder leading to the sky, so sitting on its top he imagined himself a giant. Over the years, he gradually realised how small he was compared to the universe – something like a tiny leaf in a dense forest. Although, this tininess also had a positive side – compared to the scale of the universe, unpleasant trifles lost their weight. Indeed, how could one grieve over unrequited love, about a rainy day or a morning that began with spilling tea, when compared to the universe, such problems were so tiny that even for Leeuwenhoek[26] it would have been hard to see.

---

26 Antonie Philips van Leeuwenhoek – Dutch scientist, the Father of Microbiology.

In general, he had always gravitated towards unravelling the secrets of the universe. He was sure that despite the progress of science, some things still remained unknown. For him, science was a bottomless barrel where new knowledge replaced the old, only soon to be replaced in its stead.

His attention was drawn to the children's dispute – *if God is omnipotent and immortal, can he commit suicide?* And he was greatly amused. "Only ideas can be immortal," he said to the children and offered to tell them a story. The children loved hearing his true-untrue stories, so they immediately sat around him. The man coughed to put a dividing sign between the two worlds and began.

The Tale of the Woman who Wished to be Immortal

About a hundred and fifty years ago, there lived a woman. She was an artist with all her heart and dreamed of leaving something valuable, some kind of masterpiece to the world after her death, not just a few dozen bones. She wanted people of the future to admire her art and talk about her forever. Initially, following the example of others, she tried her hand at painting, but no one liked her canvases except her husband. To tell the truth, her husband, too, wasn't particularly enthusiastic either, but he preferred to say the word "great" rather than spend hours explaining the reason why this or that piece was not great at all.

From painting she switched to literature – she wrote about her passions, and sometimes about her husband and his commercial dealings. Gradually, she switched to descriptions of landscapes, and, in the end, she even switched to philosophical topics. For instance, she wrote about whether it was worth writing at all, and even more so to write about whether it was worth writing.

"Why are you wasting your time?" her husband wondered. "The only valuable text that can be useful in life is accounting records of commercial transactions."

But still, the woman believed that one day her writings would turn out to be as crucial as the *Decameron*, and if she could not ignite the fire of passion in the hearts of people, at least she herself would become a victim of the crushing fire of the church. The woman was in a hurry, because those days no one was insured against anything. But time had a great advantage compared to her – eternity. Therefore, it annoyed her to waste time posing for her portrait only because her husband wanted to frame her youth and beauty. Her husband also struggled with time, but of course, in his own way.

At the same time, the woman also believed that on the way to glory, one canvas was not an obstacle. Even while she was sitting and posing in front of the painter, she tried not to waste time and think about future plots. Basically, she wanted to write about human passions and divine punishments caused by them; about passions because they tore her heart, and about punishments to win the heart of the clergy. "It's kind of an anti-*deus ex machina*," a painter once told her. "What do you mean?" the woman asked. "I'll tell you one story and you'll understand," the painter replied and immediately started telling his tale.

The Tale of a Man who didn't like *deus ex machina*

In Ancient Greece there lived a young playwright who had a strange quirk of creating only comedies, and this was not a tragedy for him at all. Moreover, he hated the performances in which the main characters found themselves in hopeless situations and got out of them with the help of the gods who descended to earth in their chariots. The playwright thought that the theatre was a reflection of real life and believed in it more than in gods. However, he didn't believe that the problems in real life could be solved with the help of the gods descended from heaven; consequently, for him it was *deus ex machina* that made art so unnatural and artificial.

Friends of the playwright often tried to convince him that in the theatre people liked to see the miracles which they expected to happen in life. Otherwise, why would they go there to watch what they observed in the neighbourhood every single day. Some tried to find a middle ground, arguing that people in the theatre had to see reality combining in itself the elements that would distinguish it from real life.

When friends could not convince the playwright on their own, they sent him to talk on this subject to the famous Greek sage.

"So, in your opinion, *deus ex machina* is an artificial element only for the reason that in real life the probability of its occurrence is unrealistic?" the sage asked him.

"Absolutely."

"I see. But if you don't mind, let's discuss this matter and define what real life is."

"Everything that happens around us and not what is depicted in canvases, sculptures, theatrical performances or in manuscripts."

"Although, all these things may reflect real life."

"Yes. But it's just a reflection of real life and not real life itself."

"Agreed," replied the sage. "But tell me, can we extend this assumption to other beings besides humans?"

"I don't quite understand what you mean."

"I mean, if during the performance one of the characters kills a deer, then the deer will not actually die, unlike what would happen in real life."

"Definitely."

"Or, if the canvas depicts a king mourning his dead horse, then this does not mean that the horse really died."

"Of course not."

"And if in the manuscript we read that a hedgehog…"

"Are you going to list all the fauna? Your point is already clear to me!"

"All right," said the sage, "since we agreed that the definition of real life is the same for all beings, now let's define who the gods are."

"The gods are immortal people."

"Right you are, but I'm supposed to say such things, not you, *I am* a sage. Your function is simply to agree or disagree with me, is that clear to you?"

"Yes."

"The gods also love, envy, hate, rejoice… in other words, they live like mortals, but they are immortal. Do you agree with me?"

"Didn't I say it myself?"

"Shhh! If we agree that gods are immortal humans, then can we call humans mortal gods? Because if bats are winged mice, then mice are bats without wings, and if…"

"Stop explaining with a thousand examples! One example is quite enough!"

"So, we agreed that a man is a mortal god. And to be a god means to play with the fate of those who are weaker than you. For instance, a man can kill a bird for no reason, not crush an ant, sacrifice a hundred bulls to Zeus, save…"

"I wonder how many more examples you want to give."

"That is, so far everything has been clear."

"More than clear."

"Then, tell me how many times have you saved a chick from a sudden attack by a hawk, or a fly from a web, or when you moved an ant in your palm to safety, or…"

"Never."

"Yeah? Hmm," the sage snorted, "I hope you've at least heard of such things?"

"Sure."

"Very well. Now tell me how would you define the intervention of mortal gods in the lives of living beings and changing their fate?"

"As a miracle."

"In other words?"

"Deus ex machina?" God! Is that why you started this long dialogue? I could say directly that we are gods for creatures weaker than us, and our intervention in their lives can be compared with *deus ex machina*… why do you all love sophism so much?"

"If you want to prove that you are a sage, you must either talk a lot or not utter a word," said the sage. "By the way, wisdom is needed even when asking the gods for something."

"What does this have to do with anything?"

"I know a story about it, and I would like to tell it." The sage hesitated for a moment and then added: "What sort of a sage am I if I don't tell instructive stories?"

"What's the story?" the playwright inquired. "Maybe I can use it too?"

"A long time ago…"

The Tale of the Carpenter who had to Make a Huge Toy

A long time ago, a few centuries before the ancestor of the ancestor of the ancestor of my ancestor's ancestor was born, there lived a carpenter in a certain city. He had a little son who was ill with an incurable disease. The father was ready to sacrifice his own life for the life of his son, but the gods were having fun with wars and they had no time to listen to his proposal. Three days were left before the boy would be eight years old if…

…But the carpenter didn't want to think about the "if". He was determined to fulfill every wish of his son, even if it was going to be the last one.

"I want a big toy," said the boy. "Ask the gods to give it to me, I know they are generous."

The father wanted to answer that the gods aren't always generous, especially when they send incurable diseases to children of his age or start wars, but decided to remain silent.

He still had enough wood left for the toy, so…

"Daddy, won't war prevent the gods from sending me a toy?" the son interrupted his father's thoughts.

"No. Gods always grant wishes sooner or later."

"I want sooner."

"Then I'll ask them to send you a toy before…" the father fell silent for a few seconds, "before the war ends. But you should know that the gods have one strange quality: when they give you a gift with one hand, they keep the other ready to take it away from you.

"What do you mean?" asked the child. The carpenter guessed that he had said too much, and before the boy asked him another question, he said: "I just remembered one story…"

The Tale of the Girl Abandoned by the Gods

"There lived a little girl, almost the same age as you. She lived in a beautiful distant country, where she was raised in the lap of luxury. Everyone cherished her, fulfilled her every desire, but children need friends much more than servants. Therefore, the girl made friends with a lamb, played with it all day long, and she would have gladly stayed in its stall even at night if she had been allowed to. It went on like that for a long time, until one day she couldn't find her lamb in the field when she went out to play. However, she saw her father there, who rarely played with her, and she sensed that something bad had happened. Her father was a very strict man, and he tried to raise his children strictly, because he thought that it would help them to cope with the vicissitudes of life in the future. That day the only thing he said to his daughter was that soon she would have to lose her loved ones and it was better for her to get used to the loss from an early age. The girl, of course, preferred not to start getting used to losses with the loss of her beloved animal, but her father explained to her that the lamb had a more significant role in life than just running with her.

"Can I see him one last time?" asked the girl.

"It's late," said the father, turning his eyes away from the child, and even patted her on the head to comfort her. It was so unusual that the girl forgot both the lamb and the cruelty of life for a few seconds. However, her father's hand also touched her head for only a few seconds. After that, the father went away and left the girl alone in the field.

"It's a trap!" said Memento Mori, looking at the child whose eyes filled with tears, "a literary trap…"

**

Professor Arno carefully studied the environment, but still could not establish the epoch they found themselves in. Nature has one distinctive quality – it can be absolutely the same at present and before Christ was born. True, such details as park benches, frisbees, nature conservation warnings, dogs running around in muzzles, etc., characteristic of our era, were nowhere to be seen, but it also seemed impossible to say with certainty that their absence indicated the dawn of civilisation.

"We're in the fifth layer," Memento Mori counted the stories on his fingers, and before anyone asked him how he knew, added: "A few seconds ago I finished reading and came to this conclusion."

"Why didn't you say this before?" After the last chapter,

Leah has been picking on Memeto Mori for whatever reason.

"Then it was not yet written!" Memento Mori shrugged his left shoulder and described in detail the scene that had taken place there before they arrived.

"The culmination has been already reached, hasn't it?" Matthew never liked such research. "The tyrant father used an idiotic method of upbringing, that's all. And the moral is that if we want to cope with life's adversities, we must eat a tiny bit of hot pepper every day."

Memento Mori rolled his eyes and snorted wearily, whereupon he realised that if he wanted to distance himself from participating in such ugly statements, he should never snort again.

"In my opinion, we need to look at this story from a different angle." Professor Arno came fully into play while Memento Mori was snorting. "Namely, we should think about what to add to it to turn this ordinary story into a well-known plot. We can even draw a new lamb for the girl... remind me what it's called, Inter..."

"Interstellar," Leah said.

"Intertextuality," Memento Mori replied, and Leah realised she shouldn't have mentioned *Interstellar*. "Only it will be an allusion and will not help us reach the climax."

"Maybe it's better to talk to the girl," Leah decided to take on the role of a social worker. "Such childhood traumas are fixed in the psyche and reveal themselves in adulthood. They can even cause a fatal result."

She must have heard this phrase at some conference, and it was also clear that the original source of this phrase drew it from the great experience of attending similar conferences.

Although, the synthesis of "childhood trauma" and "fatal result" pushed Memento Mori to his conclusion.

"...Revenge Is a Dish Best Served Cold." Time travel had one advantage – you could use well-known sayings before they were said by their Authors.

"How can I take revenge? He is an adult and very strong too," the girl was really too small to exact revenge and very surprised to understand the meaning of the phrase.

"Years will pass and you will definitely have the opportunity to take revenge on him. He will not even remember that he had once treated you so harshly. The problem with people is that they do not understand how much can be changed by their insignificant – at first glance – action... when Pilate was asked about Christ, he could not even recall that significant day..." Memento Mori suddenly remembered that he was talking to an eight-year-old child, who according to all the rules, had to live another twelve centuries to perceive who Christ was. "Long story short, just sit on the bank of a river and..."

...And Memento Mori suddenly realised that it was not at all necessary to recall all the known phrases about revenge. Therefore, he interrupted his phrase and instead of "Wait, your enemy's corpse will soon float by," he said just "Wait."

"All right," said the girl, and she would have wiped away her tears with her hand if this action had not been so banal. "One day he will definitely regret that he treated me so badly."

"You're a very strong girl... umm... what's your name?" Memento Mori was sure he had guessed where they were.

"Medea," the girl answered, and at the same moment everything around disappeared.

The Tale of the Carpenter who had to Make a Huge Toy

"So, is this the same girl that you told me about earlier? About the fabulous land, Golden Fleece, heroes…"

"Yes," answered the father, and stroked his son's hot forehead. "This story tells how the gods gave the King an unusual daughter, and how they themselves took her away from him with the help of Jason… and now, while they are busy with your gift, try to sleep, my boy…"

…Just at that time, eight stadiums[27] away from them, Professor Arno tried in vain to convince Memento Mori that his idea was the most primitive way to reach the climax.

"No no no! It cannot be that all time travellers who find themselves in this era did this. It would be the same as giving Herostratus a lighter while staying in Ephesus.

"I have already done it!" replied the ashamed Memento Mori. "Besides, I don't see any other way out. The emphasis here is on the gift, not on whether the boy will be saved or not. We won't reach the climax with his cure."

"But more children will die."

"Perhaps," his friendship with Machiavelli left its mark on Memento Mori, "and if you don't like it, think of something better yourselves."

This was a unique phrase that could kill any argument from the very beginning.

---

27 **Stadium** – an ancient measure of length, about 185 metres. Certainly, no one is going to remember that, and it's high time the Authors stop using measures, the meanings of which they don't often understand themselves.

"A splinter is an unpleasant thing, but it's better to let it pierce you than to sit on a hedgehog," said Matthew, though it was not clear which position he agreed with by uttering this insight. Most likely, he didn't know himself.

"By the way, in connection with the carpenter's son, I remember a completely different story, but the frequent mention of the gods in the plural tells me that we are on the right track," concluded Memento Mori and headed to the military camp at the besieged city with his hands up.

…When the rosy-fingered Eos finally woke up with saliva caked near the edge of her lip, yawned and began to touch the sky with her divine fingers, the boy also woke up. He felt good, and that terrible thing was no longer pricking him from the inside. A strange noise came in from the open window. The boy got up, looked out of the window and… oh gods!… so soon!… just in front of his house there stood his gift – a huge wooden horse.

"Dad!" the happy boy shouted, but dad did not hear him – just at the moment when he was finishing carving the wooden soldier, a spear thrown from somewhere cut his heart into two and sent him to the kingdom of Hades.

The Tale of a Man who didn't like *deus ex machina*

"Now you've finally got it, haven't you?" asked the sage.

"What?"

"Well… I don't know," the sage was confused. So much time had passed since he began telling the story that he even forgot why he started telling it.

"How strange."

"Not strange at all. People sometimes forget…"

"That's not what I meant. Look! There, high in the sky, an eagle flies with a tortoise in its talons."

"It would be strange if a tortoise flew with an eagle in its nails."

"If I were you, I would stop boasting by saying wise phrases, and would step aside."

"The wise man does not heed the advice of others; he learns from the mistakes of fools."

"So, it's time to learn from yourself."

"You're already quite insolent! Listen, if you're still here when I finish this sentence, then…"

However, the playwright did not hear what would have happened then, because the wise man, for his part, couldn't finish the sentence. It just went "BOOM!" and the playwright saw with his own eyes that the wise man had plenty of brains indeed, though not enough to protect himself against this blow.

"What can we do? Apparently, the *deus ex machina* really does not exist in real life. This was the best tragedy that the sage ever staged in his life," the playwright said, carefully walked around the body of the deceased and heard the conversation of people standing nearby: "You shouldn't have thrown that stone," said the elderly man. "Saving one tortoise cannot change the laws of nature."

"It was just a small stone," the girl was clearly taken aback. "I didn't even think I would hit the target."

"Don't worry, he would die sooner or later anyway," the young man tried to calm her down and immediately felt that it would be much better not to say anything at all.

The Tale of the Woman who Wished to be Immortal

"It still seems to me that Aeschylus did not die in this way; I mean, this reason for his death must be fictitious," said the woman. "But I didn't understand one thing – where did those people come from at the end of the story?"

"Ah, yes," the painter smiled, "for some reason, I wanted to end the story like that. In all stories there is a character who is supposedly insignificant, but in fact he is the one who moves the plot."

"Yeah, I'll write something where the minor character turns into the protagonist, if this portrait is ever completed and does not interfere with my path to fame."

"Painting is much more difficult than writing," the painter's reply sounded a little arrogant. "Why are you smiling so mysteriously?"

"Nothing serious. It's just that some people from the street are staring at me as if they see a living corpse. They resemble the characters from your story... or are they fans of my fiction?"

"I don't know, but I really like that mysterious smile of yours; it's exactly what your portrait lacks."

"The main thing is to finish it as soon as possible," the woman interrupted him. "I've got too little time for perpetuating my name."

***

"Then?" one child asked, "Did this woman become immortal?"

"Yes, but not by her writings, but thanks to just that

portrait. I saw her, and I am sure that she will remain famous for centuries."

"And why did you tell us all these stories?"

"To explain to you that eternity is sometimes obtained in a single second, and one detail can change the whole picture, is it clear to you?"

It was not clear, but since the man was known as an intelligent person, they took him at his word.

"Your fruit trees are no longer in danger, Sir. You can safely wait for our efforts to bear fruit," the gardener said as he approached the man. "It just so happened that one tree was left unsprayed, and if we don't take care of it later, its fruit may dry up prematurely."

"Leave it alone and don't worry; one apple isn't really so important."

"As you wish, Sir Isaac," mumbled the gardener, "as you wish."

***

"So, you're saying that Newton had seen the portrait of the Mona Lisa, and the trees were sprayed already in his times?" despite the time travel, Professor Arno still did not believe some matters.

"Let's agree once and for all," began Memento Mori like a character in some series, "this is another world, different from the real one, a fictitious world. Here Monet can be a simple drunkard, Degas can be a ballet dancer, and Michelangelo may not exist at all."

"Who is Michelangelo?"

"It turns out he really doesn't exist," smiled Memento

Mori. "Trust me, this whole story is made up, modelled, staged by someone. Some people invented it and now they are conducting experiments to introduce life to other planets. Historical records, archaeological excavations, fossils, cave pictographs, pyramids, great geographical discoveries, hieroglyphs, remnants of dinosaurs, people who discovered all these, historians who wrote about these people, records testifying to the existence of these historians – everything is fake. We will know the truth only when we reach the destination we are now looking for, and if we want to be saved, we must think about how to fill in the final coordinate, and not about the logical connection between the Mona Lisa and Newton."

"Where are we heading this time?" Leah tried to end the argument before it started.

"As far as I understand, meta-modernism is the next station," Memento Mori first looked at the date and only then entered the coordinates: latitude 40°44'54"N longitude 73°59'8"W + 2084. "To put it simply, we are heading back, to the Future."

Even Briefer Survey of the Planet Kimkardash

Kimkardashians don't enjoy advertising. They don't want to be brainwashed with useless information about soaps, washing powders and shampoos. Moreover, for them the products that need promotion are not worth even a toenail.[28] They believe that "any smart Kimkardashian is a walking advertisement for good products," and add that "happy Kimkardashians talk about their satisfaction to all their neighbours, while dissatisfied ones – to the whole city. So, this is the best motivation to produce good products." They also claim that "on the planet Kimkardash, no advertisement will ever bother you, which in itself is already excellent advertising."

---

28 **...are not worth even a toenail** – Some Kimkardashians do not justify using a toenail for humiliation. For them cutting the toenails is a cleansing ritual. Moreover, the Kimkardashians divide the population of their planet into two parts – those who cut off their nails without thinking, and those who leave their big toes for last.

Spoiler # 7: Atticus can't commit suicide

Advertising[29]

---

29 **Advertising** – The whole following page consists of advertisements, so
you can skip it and read on.

There were only advertisements all around: announcements, promises, discounts, billboards, posters, virtual worlds, photo offers, suggestions, words, words, words and slogans: *Live better. Divine taste. More than a swimming pool. More than just more than chocolate. Die once and get a second death with a 50% discount. The most rated GegaMegaGigaTerra show of all time. You will forget all unforgettable evenings with our beverages. Buy an apartment with a 70-year interest-free loan and suffer happily all your life. If your house has gone to the dogs, call us, go the whole hog(s)! You can get cancer any moment. So, don't waste time, insure your life today! Our quality is higher than the installment percentage. Drink our poisonous alcohol and help us become rich. Transfer all debts to our bank and suffer only in one institution. Vote for me in the elections and I will take care of the better future for myself and my family. Gain weight with our fast food. Hurry up, places are limited. Our mobile Network Operator will get you in trouble, but it will give you unlimited time to complain to your friends about us. Mongoose meat with beef flavour. Every million seven hundred and third buyer will receive a three percent discount. For the first time "For the first time in the history of mankind." Lose ten thousand in a week and get a ten euro free-bet on MacBet,* and so on and so forth.

"What the hell is going on?" Numerous visual and sound effects made Professor Arno dizzy. "Where are we?"

"Greetings to the era of commercials," Memento Mori carefully moved past the banner that took up a small part of a paragraph. "Everything here is advertising,

Dan Jackson #5
For optimism a half-empty mug is also enough

123

and advertising is everything here. It even penetrated into the only space where you never came across it directly – in books. True, commercials inserted between pages reduce the pleasure received from literature itself, but they increase profits... personally, I would never want to live in the era in which advertising is a god. The performance that sells bread! The passion for advertising is already in people's blood, in the truest sense of the word. Companies pay pregnant women to get their permission to make their embryos addicted to their brand. Accordingly, newborns already love Coca-Cola, McDonald's, Adidas, Rudens, Huxley.[30] This is a kind of investment – you pay money to parents, but you are sure that if their children are lucky in life, they will voluntarily pay the entire amount in double, or even triple... bingo! Although the main difference from our era is that here advertising is a life-threatening thing. If you listen to one of them for a long time, then it will lure you, take you prisoner and destroy you."

"Apparently, *The Odyssey* has not lost its relevance in this epoch either," smiled Professor Arno.

"I'm not kidding. Even with us, advertising is more dangerous than you think. Parallel reality. The common space of ideal worlds where there are no insoluble problems, incurable pains, stubborn stains... commercials for banks are full of happy people, but have you ever seen anyone who is happy to take out a bank loan in the world where it is much more difficult to get money than to spend it? Or how to trust the brands that scream that they want to change the world, when all they really want to change is the financial situation of their

---

30 **Rudens, Huxley** – not yet existing companies, but someday something new has to appear, after all.

owners? Do you really believe that someone somewhere really thinks about how much joy you will bring to your loved one on Valentine's Day? Of course not. They only want this joy to be caused by their products. Do you think that pharmaceutical companies are frank when they wish you good health? No, because healthy people mean their bankruptcy. Do you think anyone really wants you to live comfortably? No, because the only thing they want is to sell you an apartment, get money and create comfort for themselves. Someone somewhere invents the legend that sneakers of some company should be worn by thin people during morning exercises, and then thousands of dollars are spent to convince thin joggers to perceive it as their own privilege. In reality, in order to just do it, it doesn't matter what you wear – Adidas or Nike; Adidas shoes will not do anything for you and will not give advice on what to do either. This is all an invention of those people who do not themselves believe in what they want to convince millions of people. They offer consumers to purchase the products and services which they don't have, don't want or don't need at all, in order to get money and buy the products and services which they themselves don't have, don't want or don't need at all... nevertheless, we still cannot call advertising the art of deception; it is more the art of hiding the truth. And the truth is..." But Memento Mori couldn't say what the truth was, for all of a sudden, a huge space odyssey advertising banner emerged in front of them...

SPACE TOURS
From June 13

…And when they passed by the banner, he did not even remember where he stopped.

"Won't there happen anything else in the future apart from advertising?" Professor Arno's interest was driven more by science than marketing. "Moon tours, teleportation, Mars colonisation, alien invasions, telekinesis, telepathy…"

"You don't have to list the plots of every film about the future that you've seen," Leah commented. "Do not forget that we are just fictional characters and the future in which we find ourselves right now is also the fruit of the fantasy of one individual, some Author, who describes it in the hope that if something comes true, many years later some librarian will dig up his book and say: *Look, this guy predicted it many years ago!*" Leah was right. Therefore, Memento Mori did not say that the world had changed for the worse and that the technologies that had been created to bring people closer actually separated them more and more. That in the middle of the twenty-first century there took place a big secular schism between idealists who were for personal relationships and people addicted to tablets who were tired of the "romanticisation of relations without tablets and internet connections". The latter group, in protest, even created virtual cafes where they met with friends or with their holographic chat rooms without leaving home; that numerous emoji and stickers eventually turned into hieroglyphs and people were less and less likely to use sentences to convey something that one sticker could easily convey with a single touch of a mouse. He did not say that newborns, in order to protect themselves from the monotony of the universe, were born with white headphones fused to their heads, while the other ends of the headphones were connected to the musical device installed in their navels to make it possible to listen to music according to your mood in a continuous mode. He didn't even recall that after DNA modification, the parents themselves took after their children, which made the process of raising children something like building the saving boat for mums and dads to save them from the routine flow of their failed lives. Nor did he admit that technological advancement, with the help of hybrid surgery, had been able to connect the fingers with their gestures, and that now people could actually fire a pistol depicted by a combination of index finger and thumb; a combination of index and middle fingers created scissors to cut the nails on the other fingers; a combination of thumb and little finger created a phone which could be used to talk to anyone... the list of achievements that Memento Mori kept silent about would be longer if not for the dragon obsessed with existential problems, lying several paragraphs farther on.

"That's already too much!" Memento Mori sighed, and while he still had a chance to sigh, he began to draw up a plan. "If we want to survive, we must speak very quickly and in very short sentences, as each phrase will move us away from danger."

"If we are destined to perish here, then my last words will be…"

"If you are so verbose, then your last words will be *if we are destined to perish here, then my last words will be…*" Leah interrupted Matthew and realised that she had said a longer sentence.

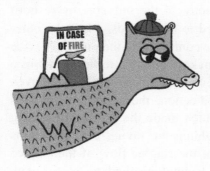

"We don't have time to argue, just talk, recall even the most meaningless phrases and words that you have ever heard!"

"You deserve someone better than me."

"Ah, are you already here?"

"I saw it, you see."

"Krrr, ja ja."

"Stud Muffin."

"Pookie."

"Boo Bear!"

"Enough!" shouted distressed Memento Mori, "I'd rather be eaten by the dragon than listen to such nonsense!"

However, the dragon was too sad to hurt anyone. He had just found out that he didn't really exist, and was simply created by an aspiring graphic artist with the help of CGI for a barbecue sauce commercial. His sadness was aggravated by the fact that no one would ever use him again for another advert, and the collapse of his career seemed as expected as accidentally putting 'like' on a post while scrolling through Facebook.

"We must find the right digit and get out of this idiotic

chapter as soon as possible!" Memento Mori left the dragon behind, looked around and found that there were only three of them.

"Despite the fact that three is more than two, yet it's not four," Matthew admitted. Professor Arno would definitely confirm this impeccable truth if he had been there…

Everyone was silent for a few seconds, and while these few seconds had not yet grown into a legitimate moment of silence, Memento Mori decided to act.

"I have to go back… maybe it's not too late. As for you two, please stay here and try not to step beyond these three asterisks."

***

"Won't anything else happen in the future apart from advertising?" Professor Arno's interest was driven more by science than marketing. "Moon tours, teleportation, Mars colonisation, alien invasions, telekinesis, telepathy…" And just at that moment, he noticed the billboard and stopped. The thirst for fame turned out to be stronger than distrust of advertising, especially since the slogan promised him what he had been dreaming of all his life – fifteen centuries of fame! Much longer than the fame of Howard Carter, William Shakespeare, Genghis Khan or even Attila could have ever been! The prospect seemed so attractive that Professor Arno unconsciously went too close to the surface of the billboard's liquid screen. "Give us fifteen minutes in exchange for fifteen centuries of fame," the inscription flickered, and from time to time, was replaced by photographs of the amazed Arno himself: Professor Arno at the grave of Queen Tamar, Professor Arno playing chess with his clone, Professor Arno – the first immortal leader of the globalised world... each photo was accompanied by headlines from the pages of well-known publications: "Professor Arnold's brilliant speech put World War IV fought with sticks and stones on hold", "The scientist who will lead the first Mayflower spacecraft to ferry people to Mars", "The archaeologist who discovered Noah's Ark with the dinosaur bones in it! Was humanity saved from starvation just thanks to dinosaur meat?" From time to time, the stills were animated and phrases were heard from the emotional speech of Professor Arno in front of a huge audience: "It is not a shame to retreat at all! This is the only thing you should never retreat from!" "We can move to Mars at any time, but it's much easier to save the Earth so that we don't have to move to Mars." "An alien is not always an enemy, just as an earthling is not always a friend..." Professor Arno came closer and closer to the screen. Fame had never been as accessible as it was now. Just three steps. Nobel Prize. Discovery of Atlantis. The cold-blooded enemy of global warming. Two steps. Ruler of the world. First man on Pluto. Inventor of the immortality vaccine. One step. One small step for a man, which would be a giant leap for mankind. Books, magazines, films, speeches mingled with one another. It was the Brave New World beyond The Doors of Perception. With one foot he had already stepped onto the viscous surface of the screen. There was very little left, very little! And just as he was about to jump into the whirlpool of glory, someone grabbed him by the shoulder, and with a strong movement, threw him back over the three asterisks.

***

Leah and Matthew were standing under the glittering asterisks, but before Matthew dared to say: "How romantic, isn't it?" Professor Arno flew like a bullet over their heads. Suddenly, everything changed: buildings began to grow out of the ground with lightning speed, as if some giant was playing Tetris in an accelerated mode. Military helicopters were humming in the sky. People appearing out of nowhere were screaming and running back and forth through the streets in a very strange way. Traffic stopped. And before Matthew could ask what the hell was going on, he was gently grabbed by a huge hand…

…The first thing Professor Arno saw after he came to his senses was a huge monkey. He held Matthew in one hand, and with the help of the other hurriedly climbed a building that looked a lot like the Empire State Building. Boys in blue fired in vain from helicopters. "A midge very rarely gets a chance to avenge its prematurely crushed brethren," Professor Arno thought instead of Matthew, because when someone is trapped in a huge hairy hand, such phrases hardly come to their mind. Matthew himself was about to shout out to Leah that he seemed to love her, when King Kong dropped the last helicopter, climbed to the top of the Empire State Building and yelled intimidatingly. He opened his hand…

"…And then, let him treat the boy to our beer, open the bottle with his teeth, put him on his shoulder and they will admire the sunset together. This romantic King Kong will be the new big thing. Yeah! Everyone will definitely share it… you can even change the slogan with something

like: *When you are thirsty for adventure,* or *Quench your thirst!* Or no, no... it will look like bestiality... no problem anyway, we can come up with the slogan later."

"Umm," said the aged marketing manager for a beer company, "these are the kind of ads I saw as a kid in the twenties. Why do we have to start over at the end of the twenty-first century?

"Who are we going to surprise today with romantic King Kong and all sorts of monkey tricks? But on the whole, I like that the ads are interactive and that King Kong takes different men every time... good experience... therefore, we can still try it... but this depressive dragon and all this blah blah before that is definitely not useful... well, of course, it's good to make fun of other advertisements in your advertising, but still... it all increases a film's duration and people get tired of watching."

...While King Kong brought Matthew back and disappeared until the next commercial insert, Memento Mori already had a new plan – he had to find the ideal character to somehow calm the Author. It had to be someone whose death would sadden the reader, because playing on the reader's emotions was a good bait for any Author.

"So, you want to sacrifice some literary Bruce Willis to the Author while we are saving the world," Matthew concluded.

"Exactly. Otherwise, it will be difficult for us to find two necessary lacking parts of the coordinate in the given situation... but the problem is that neither is it easy to find the ideal character."

"Umm," uttered Leah. But as solely this interjection expressed nothing significant, she added: "There is a book,

I'm sure you don't know it, which describes a situation in which you are sure to find an ideal candidate."

"What situation do you mean?"

"Umm," uttered Leah again. But as this interjection couldn't express anything significant again, she again added: "Literary Hell…"

Spoiler # 8: Noman Escapes from Comics

Hemingway lived on a calm street. Quiet, cosy and peaceful street of synonyms. A small room was enough for him. With a typewriter and an old fireplace. On the right of the fireplace. There hung his quarry. On the left an old gun. A gift from Chekhov. A stuffed mockingbird stood on the mantlepiece. Hemingway did not like to talk much. Or rather he could not. This was his punishment in literary hell. His sentences could consist of only seven words at most. He was fired from television. Just for this simple reason. He spoke too clearly for a journalist. Only after that, he learned the language of weapons. He hunted in Sherwood Forest. Or somewhere nearby. He hunted for Electric Sheep or Steppenwolves. Until everything had changed…

***

Virginia Woolf said she would pick the flowers herself. At the edge of Sherwood Forest, the violets had already cut through the ground. It seemed they were striving for heaven, but their roots would not let them go. If Virginia had been a poetess, she would have written a poem about a gardener cutting a violet with a bayonet, and synthesising the tenderness of a violet with the aggressiveness of a bayonet, she would get a good poetic image. But Virginia was not a poet. She just loved the fields dotted with violets. And she also loved Sylvia – the permanent source of the immortality of butterflies in her belly and the only prisoner of all four chambers of her heart. She knew that when Sylvia woke up, she would be glad to see flowers. Or rather, not the flowers, but the manifestation of care shown to her. Ever since public outrage had kept them both in the bell jar, she had become a goddess of small things and tried to influence Sylvia's spirits with such tiny details. She did not give a damn about the mocking gazes of her neighbours and the exclamations of writers of the Victorian Era: *Let them do what they want in their room, but not in front of our eyes!* "Actually, society is just a euphemism for the masses," thought Virginia. "If you want to achieve something in life, never listen to those who say that in this way you will not achieve anything."

Virginia quickly crossed Alexanderplatz and stopped at the tracks. She waited for the Streetcar Named Desire to pass by. Ever since Anushka's negligence caused Professor Dowell's accident, she had tried to be cautious. Caution was just a dandelion in a glass jar. She crossed the tracks, walked five paces to the northeast, and quickly passed the *Buddenbrokers* – the currency exchange office decorated with a thousand light bulbs that illuminated the entire literary hell. "Piastres, piastres, piastres," she heard the irritating shouts from the building, whereupon she took three more steps perpendicular to the building and followed the lane of Cormac McCarthy. Then, she would turn to the right, go to Mérimée Avenue, and after taking another sixty-seven steps she would have got to the forest. "Everything will pass," said Virginia, "Oscar Wilde was not honoured at first either." Seven short steps to the southeast. Three long steps to the west. She stepped on the pavement and hardly escaped from crashing 103683, sleeping in the shade of the grass a few centimetres away. There were still twenty-seven steps left before the turn. Two, three, four. How strange – people learn to walk from an early age, but some cannot take a decisive step all their lives. Nine, ten. Far away, at the Headless Horseman's Headquarters, she spotted Hemingway. After being fired from the Big Brother Channel, he lived a carefree life. In the mornings he hunted for animals, and he drank every single night – quarts, pints, litres. It seemed he had a Danaid bathtub instead of stomach. His hands were trembling from drinking. Therefore, when he cocked the trigger, everyone ran away except for the animal he was aiming at. Twenty-two. Twenty-three. Twenty-four. Twenty-five. Twenty-six. Twenty-seven.

She turned the corner.

***

"So, which book were you talking about?" Memento Mori looked around.

"*Bestseller* – a satirical-parodic-detective-puzzling-fantasy-science fiction-etc. novel about a literary hell where famous and unknown writers are tormented in the same way as they have tormented their readers…" Leah said it so quickly that even Jesse Owens couldn't have enough time to run sixty metres.

"Wow, did you learn it by heart?"

"No. Simply, for the last four years, wherever its Author appears, he doesn't say anything else," Leah justified herself either because of her own bad memory, or because of the Author's stereotype, and passed by the workshop of Joyce's footnotes...[31]

...The street led to Oxymoron Square, between the monuments of Noisy Solitude and White Nights. In this part of the Vanity Fair, there was a forge of Dostoevsky's ideal characters... Leah and Memento Mori were alone. Matthew and Professor Arno refused to meet the classic Author. One went to look for Conan Doyle, and the other to find his happiness. Leah also wanted to take a good look at literary hell, but first she had to take a selfie with Dostoyevsky. True, only an idiot would have believed her that in the photo there really was Dostoevsky and not his double, but she would worry about it later.

"So which character do you like better?" Dostoevsky leafed through a very thick catalogue. His crime was the creation of perfect characters for which he received the proper punishment. "Someone who struggles with life or the humble one? The rounded character who goes through the spiritual changes or the flat one who always remains the same? The protagonist who becomes the antagonist or vice versa?"

"We need a character whose death will sadden the reader."

"Then let's pick up something fashionable," Dostoevsky opened the catalogue to the letter **T** and ran his finger over the word **Trendy.** "If you want someone a bit poetic, then this girl will suit you. Thin as a layer of jam on bread and butter, and

---

31 **Workshop of Joyce's footnotes** – a place in the literary hell where Joyce makes up footnotes for his own footnotes.

transparent as a drop of spring rain hanging on an acacia thorn. Her hair is wavy like the sea which she fed with her tears all her life. Her heart is so full of love that not only butterflies are found in her stomach, but also larvae and pupae. For her love is like a hot coal that can either go out or turn into a big fire..."

"No no, we already have one like that," said Memento Mori.

"Who?" inquired Leah, but no one answered.

"Then what about this rebellious character, who believes that every politician should be burned at the stake kindled by their own chairs; that the only good deed of the generation of fathers is the creation of his generation; that getting drunk is not an option, and if you still have to drink, a Molotov cocktail will do for this... many people like such characters."

"But their deaths won't come as a surprise."

"Hmm. And if you try a brilliant child of six or seven, who actually has absorbed all the Author's life wisdom? A few sharp observations on the adult world will be enough, for example: "adults are constantly trying to make robots look like people, but in reality, they turn into robots themselves", or, "cars are like predatory animals – every morning they stretch and go hunting in the concrete jungle," or: "why do people think that the god who created the whole world needs their protection?" They immediately become favourites – adults adore children who think like adults..."

"I hope you won't agree to kill a child and violate his constitutional rights," Leah whispered in Memento Mori's ear and prepared to confront him.

"Then opt for a vegetarian," Dostoevsky had more choices, but he was very tired. "I can't recommend anything trendier."

"And how are they different besides being vegetarian? What else do they do to be considered perfect?"

"Is vegetarianism not enough?" Dostoevsky was surprised in all sincerity. "I think that's quite enough."

***

The real purpose of Professor Arno's promenade was to avoid sightseeing in literary hell. For a person who wanted to come up with good final words, this place was a true paradise. Where else could he have found the better society of dead writers and poets? The professor believed that in order to urgently come up with ideal sentences, even the status of a writer was sufficient, but he did not know that even the simplest sentences, which emphasised his overestimated idea of the skills of writers, were processed several times by the Author himself and then by the editor and proofreader. He believed that the final words should have been short, exclusive and sentimental, such as "For sale: baby shoes, never worn"[32] proved to be. Therefore, as soon as The Sun also Rose, Arno started looking for Hemingway. He did not find him at home. Some writer looking like Abraham Lincoln who broke the razor while shaving his beard[33] readily told him that Hemingway was to be found in the woods. Arno roughly calculated the location of Sherwood Forest, and without any fear and repidation, headed there. Because of the

32 **For sale: baby shoes, never worn** – Hemingway's story consisting of six words.
33 **Abraham Lincoln who broke his razor while shaving his beard** – writer Henry David Thoreau. But no one is obliged to know his appearance, so let's not scold Professor Arno for not recognising him (Author's sincere request).

early morning the streets were almost deserted. Only someone with a familiar face stood nearby whitewashing the fence:

"Excuse me, is this the right way to Sherwood Forest?"

No answer.

"Excuse me, is this the right way to Sherwood Forest?" Arno repeated the question.

No answer again.

"Go to the end of the street and then turn left," Professor Arnaud heard a voice from a completely different direction. He turned around and noticed a strangely dressed long-nosed man in a red cap and a laurel wreath on his head. He was accompanied by two confused companions. One of them was Umberto Eco, but the Professor did not recognise the woman.

"If a person does not read books, then he should at least look at the back cover," thought Professor, and before he began self-torture due to ignorance of what the Authors looked like, he headed in the indicated direction. From behind he still heard the words of the strangely dressed guide: "That's where Shakespeare's hotel *Hothello* is…"

***

Hemingway dreamed of lions all night. (Hunting in Narnia has already become his cherished dream.) Sherwood was too small for him. Therefore, he went there. Only out of habit. These short sentences. Also got on his nerves. He tried several times. To say longer sentences. But the full stop always. Appeared in an unusual place. And didn't give him the opportunity. To complete the thought. In literary hell, the sun rose lazily. Hemingway put on a red baseball cap. Suddenly, he heard a familiar sound. A flock of a thousand cranes. Flew over him. They flew like a bullet. Over a rye field. Bullets would never catch up with them.

Hemingway took a few steps. Towards the forest. He saw Virginia Woolf. In the field spotted with violets. Everyone has been talking about her lately. About her and Sylvia Plath. "Beauvoir has corrupted them," he thought. "A woman no longer looks like a woman," he added. "Ugh! And this thirty-year difference!... no, such debauchery was unbearable! A stray bullet would solve everything. One shot and she would fly to Nangijala. To Lindgren's isolated paradise in hell." Two bottles of whiskey gave him courage. He adjusted his baseball cap nicely. The big-game hunt for Virginia Woolf began.

***

"Let it be him," said Memento Mori after eleven minutes' reflection.

"Atticus! An excellent choice," agreed Dostoevsky. He was already so tired that he would even approve of Frankenstein's monster. "Atticus is just. Kind. Protects the oppressed. If all novels had at least one such ideal character, many more people would love literature... I will serve him to you right away, but I want to warn you that a sold character is never accepted back."

"If he's so perfect, why should we return him?" Memento Mori was surprised.

"All perfect characters have one flaw, you see."

"What's the flaw?"

"See for yourself," muttered Dostoevsky, and handed him

a two-hundred-and-fifty-page manual along with the warranty card. "It must be written somewhere there…"

***

Looking at Hemingway, Professor Arno immediately regretted that he had not read any of his works. What could he do? He did not like to read fiction; especially after Elsa's death. She was a real bookworm. When she began to read a novel, she read it avidly. She said that it was very unfair to stop reading when the characters were in a difficult situation, because you doomed them to endless torment until you felt like continuing. The only book she didn't read to the end was the one she read on the last night of her life. Arno still remembered the name of the book – *The Castle*. But he could not remember Elsa's last words; she either said: "if Kafka had not died so young, he would probably have written many more masterpieces", or: "I feel bad, can you give me a glass of water?" But of these two, he himself certainly would not have chosen either. "I wonder what words Hemingway himself uttered before he died?" thought Arno. "Or what would I say in his place before pulling the trigger? At least…" and suddenly the Professor guessed what he would say. Everything turned out to be very simple. For so many years he thought about what could be guessed by thinking about what another person would do. "Great! Now I can safely look death in the eye!" he whispered, and only then did he notice an unfamiliar woman squatting down twenty paces from him. Virginia Woolf bent down to pick another violet. "Life is like a flower," she thought. "You grow and bloom, you believe that you are moving away from the ground more and more, but all this is an illusion. The ground will never let you go far..." and having picked a few flowers, she saw a gun aiming at her.

Hemingway's head was heavy from alcohol. "Man is a wolf to man," he said cruelly. Trembling hand. Cocked trigger. Virginia Woolf was petrified with fear. She guessed she only had hours, if not minutes or seconds, left.

The sound of the gunshot scared the crows.

Virginia didn't move. She knew that Hemingway's hands were trembling and whenever he cocked the trigger, everyone ran away except for the beast he was aiming at. Therefore, she did not feel pain; she simply heard that somewhere nearby someone fell down. Only now did she notice that there was a third person next to them. An elderly man. With a white beard stained in places with drops of blood. A lot of full stops marking the end of his life. The stunned Hemingway sobered up. He dropped his weapon and ran towards the forest. Virginia was confused too. She did not know what to do in such a case. She was twelve steps away from the stranger. One, two, three. She walked closer to him. Four, five, six. Maybe it was better to call someone for help? Seven, eight, nine. Life is short-lived and fragile, like a toy on a Christmas tree. Ten, eleven, twelve. Surprise was written on the man's face. The bullet hit him right in the neck and tore it apart. He moved his lips languidly. "He wants to say something," thought Virginia. "The final words try to free themselves from the imprisonment of the tongue."

"Hem... hemmm... em... em..." Professor Arno tried to clear his throat and departed into the other world without uttering a single word. "Life is really like a flower," said

Virginia sadly and stroked the old man's head. "Even when it's completely faded, it's still a pity to throw it away…"

***

Memento Mori felt absolutely worthless – the Author was one step ahead of him again.

"And the worst part is," he added, "that nobody would write a book about the senseless death of an ordinary Professor. The alarm clock is counting the hours of a completely different person."

Memento Mori and Matthew stood at the crossroads of the Red and Black Squares. Quite recently, feminist writers protested there against the "frequent facts of physical and spiritual violence against women by alcoholic schizoids." Leah, most likely, should have been there too, but she was nowhere to be seen. Only banners were scattered around: "Go to sea, no place for old men here." "Hello weapons." "More women in literary hell", etc.

"Excuse me, have you seen a strange girl here?" asked Memento Mori and immediately guessed that the wording of this question sounded exactly the same as the question "have you seen Buendia?" would sound in Macondo.

"There was only one unfamiliar girl here," replied some writer whom neither Memento Mori nor Matthew, and probably not even the readers knew. "She found fault with Zola for his novel "Women's Happiness", then suddenly disappeared and this sheet appeared in her place.

"Things are getting more and more confusing!" *yelled* Memento Mori because such sentences could not be simply *said*. "Well, Mr. Detective, it's time for you to come into the play…"

"I am a detective, not Shampolion," Matthew guessed that he didn't pronounce the last name correctly… but what could he do? He not only didn't remember the person's first name, but did not know it at all. "Champalion, Champollion or whatever."

"Ugh! Severe deficiency of little grey cells…" *said* Memento Mori, as *ironically remarked* was out of place in the given circumstances. Even a child could easily solve this puzzle.[34] Actually, it is a hastily drawn Don Quixote, not a hieroglyph. Apparently, the Author decided to play a literary game with us."

"Literature is not my forte."

"Then, just try not to disturb me," *replied* Memento Mori, as the verbs *berated* or *scolded* sounded pretty inappropriate to him. "Time to leave this chapter and follow the directions…"

---

34 **Even a child could easily solve this puzzle** – If you are a child and are not able to solve it, take it easy, because it's a figurative phrase invented by adults without children's permission (The Authors soothing note).

In Search of Lost Leah

Chapter 1

This describes how Matthew and Memento Mori went around all of La Mancha; how they came across a wandering knight who mistook them for Orlando Furioso and his squire; how a fierce fight between them took place; how Sancho Panza separated the fighting parties before something terrible had happened; how they held a great feast in a nearby tavern; how night came, then morning, and night again; how it dawned on them about where Leah could be; how Memento Mori found a drawing in the tavern with images of a cloud, rain, and the sign of infinity; how he decided that this place was very similar to Macondo; how afterwards the Author thought that it was pointless to write this chapter, since everything was already said in the title, and moved on directly to the next one.

Chapter 2 – It's Raining in Macondo

A few paragraphs will pass, and soaked to the skin Memento Mori, standing in an old kitchen, will find out that José Arcadio Buendia, Aureliano José Buendia, Arcadio José

Buendia and Arcadio Aureliano Buendia are different people. Until then, it will rain torrentially, and non-stop. "This is magical realism and everything that usually happens in dreams can happen in reality here," Memento Mori will say, and just at that moment a blind old man named Jorge Luis, holding a sand umbrella in one hand, will appear from the veil of rain. "You are looking for someone very special to you in the labyrinths of literature," he will smile. "Wow, did you really spend all that time coming to such a conclusion?" Matthew will answer and immediately guess that his answer does not quite fit the general style of the narration. "Searching in Macondo is a futile effort," the blind old man will add, then turn into sand himself and dissolve into the rain along with his umbrella.

Then Three Men in a Boat (To Say Nothing of the Dog) will come. "Damn it! We escaped from London just because of the rain," one of the men, who will be rowing with spoons instead of oars will say ruefully, and will tell the story of a girl who appeared in Macondo many letter-sounds ago, and who had very, very, very, very long, longer than this sentence hair. She was accompanied by a guy called Author, who was holding a device similar to a suitcase with buttons. "It's a laptop," Matthew will say, but meanwhile the boat will spread wings and fly away.

It won't stop raining and soon there will emerge a house with a thatch roof. A soaked sheet of paper will be glued on the door of the house, and on the paper, there will be a blurry inscription DOOR . Behind the door there will be a table with an inscription TABLE glued to it. There will be chairs around the table, and the inscription CHAIR will be glued to each. Men will be sitting on those chairs, and they will have inscriptions glued on their foreheads: JOSÉ ARCADIO , AURELIANO JOSÉ , ARCADIO JOSÉ , ARCADIO AURELIANO . And Memento Mori will find out that José Arcadio Buendia, Aureliano José Buendia, Arcadio José Buendia and Arcadio Aureliano Buendia are different people. "Are they playing a *game of guessing who you are*, or what?" Matthew will inquire, and Memento Mori will remember that once, in Macondo, people forgot all the words from lack of sleep. "We are looking for a woman with very, very, very, very long, longer than this sentence hair," Memento Mori will say. "Hair?" Aureliano José will strain his memory and pass his hand over his forelock. "I vaguely remember…" "Look at the refrigerator! There is a drawing in exactly the same style as the one we are looking for!" Matthew will cry out and again guess that his utterance does not quite fit the general style of narration. Out of the kitchen door with the inscription KITCHEN DOOR , a man will appear with a thick gray moustache and southern looks. "What makes you think that I write in such a strange manner?" he will be angry. "Now stop using this inappropriate tense and get the hell out of here!" And on the paper, there will be drawn a rabbit and a tongue sticking out of someone's beard. "It's Aesop's tongue," Matthew will say, and it will be so unexpected from him that he himself will believe in the real magic of magical realism.

A few more letters will pass, and Memento Mori will no longer be here.

Chapter 3 – The Hare and the Fox

One hare decided to become an artist. He smeared something with charcoal on the bark of trees, and since no one had ever seen real paintings, everyone liked his works. The name of the hare became famous for its weight in the forest, and he became so bold that he stopped shunning even predators.

Once a fox visited him and asked to draw his portrait. "It's not a difficult task," said the hare. "Of course, it's very easy," agreed the fox; "It would be much more difficult if you drew with one eye closed." "Nothing like that, it's not difficult either," answered the hare, closed one eye and continued to draw. "You were right," the fox agreed. "But you would be a real master, if you can draw with two eyes closed." "I can do it," the hare replied proudly and closed both eyes. The fox was just waiting for this – she calmly caught the hare and carried it away to her hole.

"The moral of the fable is that you don't have to be stupid," said Memento Mori, who appeared from somewhere, took the drawing and scrutinised it for a while. "I don't really understand why the fox arranged such an operation to catch one hare, but in my opinion, I look more like a hydraulic press piston valve than this drawing looks like a fox."

Chapter 4 – The Time[35]

There was a sunset in Europe.[36]

"We, people are always in search of lost time.[37] For us, time is like a cracked vessel full of water, which is constantly leaking: plink, plink, plink. It doesn't matter what we are doing – drinking beer, listening to music or smoking a cigar,[38] this plinking never stops. However, it's all our fault. We ourselves came up with the idea that one rotation of the earth around the sun is one year, and by enclosing ourselves in a frame of time, we enclosed ourselves in a hamster wheel – going forward and remaining in place simultaneously. Even this metaphor with the hamster wheel hasn't changed in years. Every year, at the same time, we perform the same ritual and think that

---

35 **Time** – the title is so profound and all-encompassing that a couple of footnotes won't even be enough to explain it.

36 **There was a sunset in Europe** – alluding to "The Decline of the West", the title of a well-known work by Oswald Spengler in which he speaks of the downturn of European civilisation and echoes Hegel's work on several stages of civilisation, where the sunset of Europe can be identified with the twilight in Faust's study.

Hegel – a famous German philosopher. The names of such famous philosophers as Hölderlin and Heideger also start with the same letter.

Faust – a legendary character about whom Goethe wrote a tragic play in two parts only for the majority of people to remember one single phrase from it: "Stop, moment, you are wonderful!"

37 **In Search of Lost Time** – a very direct and rather weak association with Proust. Consequently, it can be concluded that the Author is familiar only with the title of this well-known cycle of Proust's works (as well as with the fact that this is not one work but a series of works). Although, all this has been made clear in the second paragraph of the first prologue of this book.

38 **Beer, music, cigar** – a paraphrase of Nietzsche's phrase, but which one exactly, only God knows.

life is arranged so… that's why history is a farce;[39] a constant repetition. And if we really want to subdue time, then change is needed. Change is the enemy of monotony. It[40] fearlessly fights against such dangerous words as "forever" and "never". You understand how stupid it is to say to someone "I will love you forever" or "I will never leave you", because by saying this you doom both yourself and the partner to terrible monotony…"

"We're wasting time," Memento Mori interrupted him, carefully looked at one sketch of Hofrat  Behrens, and deported Matthew from one world to another so that the detective himself did not guess why such thoughts came to his mind.[41]

Chapter 5 – No!

Happy families are all alike, and unhappy couples are also alike. Matthew did not believe that in order to love someone, one had to suffer for seven hundred pages. "Why couldn't Leah just fall in love with me without any prerequisites," he thought.

"It just won't work out that way. There are rules of genre,

---

39 **That's why history is a farce** – a modification of a phrase by Marx that someone else, such as Hegel, might have said before him.

40 **It** – in his work "Totem and Taboo" S. Freud uses this word more than once.

41 **…such thoughts came to his mind** – there is nothing incomprehensible in this sentence. This footnote merely serves to increase the number of ambiguous phrases that need explanation, and thereby create the impression that you are reading a very sophisticated piece.

structure, plot, this and that," answered Memento Mori.

Matthew was at first confused, then frightened. Or vice versa – first, he was frightened and next confused, because he was so confused or frightened that he did not find the strength in himself to establish the sequence of fright and confusion. He had no idea that Memento Mori could read his mind!

"I have nothing to do with it," Memento Mori justified himself. "This is the era of the omnipotent Author. And, as you know, he can not only read thoughts, but also transmit them. I just read the thoughts that have already been depicted by him.

And Matthew guessed that he had a unique chance to bargain with the Author about his love for Leah. Naturally, he was also aware that the addressee of his request already knew what Matthew wanted, which gave him some advantage during the bargaining. But because of this detail, he was not going to miss a great chance to establish direct contact with the Author.

"Hey!" he said, as he did not know how to address the Author. "I beg you, let Leah fall in love with me... or rather, I ask you to give us the opportunity to find her first, and then let her fall in love with me... I know that for you it's like shelling peas; you must only write one short sentence – *she fell in love with him* – and then you don't have to mention me at all. Don't think about genre, plot, and so on. People adore love stories and everyone will be happy. Besides, imagine how many people will have the hope that sometimes miracles do happen... come on, come on..."

Frozen in anticipation of some kind of sign, Matthew began to survey the surroundings. They were standing in front of a huge redbrick house. On one side the building was surrounded by a fence of beech trees, and on the other by a wall of hewn stones. Cherry trees were blooming in the orchard, and the air was filled with the smell of early spring, saturated with the fragrance of crushed elderberry. Bees buzzed over the newly blossomed buds, and under the fence, snowdrops proudly raised their heads. A train whistle was heard from afar.

"Send me a dove at least, do something, give me a sign," Matthew was losing patience.

And a dove really came down from heaven, but instead of an olive branch, he was holding a piece of paper.

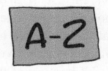

"A-Z," Matthew read aloud, "what does it mean?"

"It's a completely different thing," Memento Mori was too lazy to explain, otherwise he would have said that these two letters stood for an encyclopedia. "Maybe your answer is written on the other side."

"This is what's written there, nothing more."

Chapter 6 – A-Z

Mori, Memento. Born in Another Prologue. Date of birth unknown. A character in the book *Everyone Dies in this*

Novel. Warns other characters of an expected danger. Hence his name, which in Latin means 'remember death'. Over the years, Memento Mori travelled in many books. It was he who helped Baron Munchausen get out of the swamp (which later found itself in many different legends). He led the rescue operation to free Little Red Riding Hood from the belly of a wolf. For many years he secretly helped Robinson Crusoe, Captain Nemo, Count Monte Cristo and many others. He has the ability to read the text that is written around him and even travel in it. He believes that the wiser and wittier the last phrase of a paragraph, the easier the whole paragraph is remembered, which can hardly be said about this paragraph.

Matthew is a false detective, a character in the book *Everyone Dies in this Novel*. Distinguished by his useless ideas. For example, he believes that the best place to choose a religion is in a turbulent zone. And to get rid of unnecessary stress, you need to fall in love with someone whose birthday is not scheduled for the next six months. And he also thinks that in order to contrast with the rappers' repertoire, the rockers' repertoire should be called Rockertoire etc. He hates writers who use spoilers, such as: 'They could not imagine that this was their last meeting' or 'When Joseph woke up, he did not yet know that he would die that day.' If Matthew loved such phrases, he might not have died by the end of the book.

I'm kidding, of course.

Or, maybe, not.

Leah – daughter of Laban. Rachel's sister.

Chapter 7 – Genesis 29

16. Now Laban had two daughters: the name of the older was Leah, and the name of the younger was Rachel.

17. Leah had weak eyes, but Rachel had a lovely figure and was beautiful.

18. Jacob was in love with Rachel and said to Laban, "I'll work for you for seven years in return for your younger daughter Rachel."

19. Laban replied, "It's better that I give her to you than to some other man. Stay here with me."

20. So Jacob worked seven years to get Rachel, but they seemed like only a few days to him because of his love for her.

21. Then Jacob said to Laban, "Give me my wife. My time is completed, and I want to make love to her."

22. So Laban brought together all the people of the place and gave a feast.

23. But when evening came, he took his daughter Leah and brought her to Jacob, and Jacob entered the room to make love to his wife.[42]

24. And in the room was a man instead of the woman. And the man said, "My name is Memento Mori."

25. And Jacob said, "What do you want?"

26. And Memento Mori said, "I want Leah back. It is not necessary to have eighty-seven children."

27. Then Jacob said to Memento Mori, "Take Leah back, I love Rachel."

28. And when Leah entered, Memento Mori was

---

42 16-23 – passages from the new version of the Old Testament. As for this footnote, it is given because the same holy scripture says: do not steal.

astonished: it was not his Leah.

29. And Memento Mori said to Jacob, "I beg your pardon, I was deceived too... it will be nice if you omit this episode in Genesis."

30. "Which Genesis?" Jacob asked.

31. And Memento Mori added: "As well as the list who gave birth to whom. Nobody is interested in genealogical trees of the people living five thousand years ago. So, nobody will ever read those chapters. Marry Rachel and take care of Joseph."

32. And Jacob said to Memento Mori, "Who is Joseph? What do you have to do with my future?"

33. But Memento Mori had already gone.

Chapter 8 – The Planet of the Little Prince

B-612 was completely deserted. Only baobabs spread around and the surface of the planet was covered with volcanic ash. In its centre, a glass globe was barely visible, with faded rose petals under it.

"Why did we come here?" Matthew was overcome by the same feeling he had during the last episode of *Friends*.

"I have nothing to do with it," Memento Mori replied in confusion. "Maybe the Author decided to add this scene to say while advertising his novel that the characters are travelling on the planet of the Little Prince. A lot of people will buy the book just because of this detail.

"Actually, a ruined planet awaits them."

"Nothing can be done! I did my best, but the snake venom was too poisonous," Memento Mori didn't look very sad. "Maybe it was even better that way, because a few years later, a worse thing would be inevitable, and it would be even more difficult to come to terms with that – the Little Prince would have become an adult and forgotten the time when he was a child.

They stood in silence for several minutes. The silence that reigned on the planet was broken only by the immortal melody of John Cage.

"And Leah... he didn't kill her, did he?" Matthew nevertheless raised the question that both were afraid of.

"I don't think he'll take that risk."

"What's the risk?"

"Killing the activist. In this case, they will say about him that he is misogynistic, subconsciously hates women, there was only one woman in the book and he could not stand it."

"And why is he hiding her? Maybe he wants the reader to be in two minds, not knowing whether she is alive or not, like Erwin Schrödinger's animal... umm... whatever it is..."

"I don't know really. Then why is he leaving clues?"

"Now there aren't even any clues."

"Maybe the fact that we have no clues *is* the main clue?"

"Well done, bravo! It all became clear right away..." said Matthew, because the dialogue had been going on for some time without explaining which of the two of them was speaking, and soon the reader would have to figure it out for themselves, starting from the phrase 'nevertheless raised the question that both were afraid of'. "We must do something; we can't just sit and wait."

"Firstly, we can sit and wait, and secondly, this is a great idea!"

"What?"

"It's a fact that only the two of us are left in the entire book. If we remain silent and inactive, the Author will have to write the next chapter about Leah. And thus, we will at least find out where she is."

Matthew couldn't think of anything smarter than that, so they just sat under one baobab tree and enjoyed the sunset.

Chapter 9 – The Forty Rules of Suicide

Atticus was fond of formulating conspiracy theories. For instance, he believed that the main reason for the creation of Santa Claus was to accustom children to the existence of God and obedience to him from early childhood, since for adults, God was nothing but Santa Claus – a bearded creature that no one has ever seen anywhere except in films, and who fulfils your desires only when you behave well and do nothing offensive. It surprised him that adults who were always amused by the children's naïve belief in the existence of Santa, sometimes even killed each other in the name of God. Gradually, he began to try to turn his theories into anthropological conclusions, and with luck, even to find such a correlation, which would later be called by his name. "We tend to find a connection between negative phenomena and ourselves more often than with positive ones," he said. "For example: if a rumor spreads that a young man has drowned in the seaside town of N, where our son is staying, we will immediately call him to make sure that he is alive, whereas if in the same town a young man wins a million, it is very unlikely that we'll think the winner is our son. Or why do we persistently ask about the cause of death of the deceased? Because we want to clarify whether we are in the same danger or not." True, these observations and arguments were not ideal, and no one would have named anything in honour of someone's name, but Atticus was still pleased with himself, since ideal people can be content with even a little.

The bad news was that in spite of all this, Atticus still had to die. In an ideal world, killing characters might not be the only means of exciting the reader's emotions, but unfortunately in this case, Atticus himself was ideal, and not the world around him. However, to obtain the desired effect, it was first necessary to win the sympathy of the reader... "I, somehow, must show my high moral standards and ascribe to myself many decisive pluses in the eyes of the reader," thought Atticus and smiled while gently caressing the cat that appeared from somewhere. He really loved animals very much (+). True, when saying that they loved animals, people often meant love for their meat, but Atticus tried to embody the idea of universal vegetarianism (+), and whenever he did not think about practical steps that needed to be taken to reduce global warming (+), he continued to work on a large-scale project to save endangered species (+). By and by he realised that people were not in hot pursuit of global warming, and switched to the local problems: he fought against gender stereotypes in promotions. He set out to destroy the notion that a washing machine, iron and various kitchen appliances were gifts created specifically for women (+). He did not smoke (+). He drank moderately (+). If his friends didn't look good in photos, he didn't upload those photos without their permission (+). He expressed his opinion only about those things that he knew and understood well, and did not pass himself off as an expert in all matters, from the basics of the fight against terrorism to the claim to create the only, vital and firm model for saving the country's economy, the details of which, to tell the truth, he did not understand at all (+). When he talked to people, he really listened to them (+). Moreover, after each of their proposals, he did not start telling stories about himself with the words "By the way, in connection with this, I remembered... (+). He had lots of other pluses too (+) and his only minus was that he was perfect... or rather, he thought he was perfect, since actually, in the second paragraph on page ninety of his two-hundred-and-fifty-page manual, it was written: "...although, being perfect is a bit boring and can even cause depression. Life is really interesting because people are not perfect and break those little rules that they themselves have established. For those who are deprived of such pleasures, even the desire to live may disappear..." Therefore, when forging Atticus, Dostoevsky made it so that he could never commit suicide. It was only after three unsuccessful attempts that Atticus realised that not everything was as perfect as he thought. Neither the pills nor the bullet helped his problem. Moreover, when he threw himself into the river, he found out that he could breathe freely underwater. Nothing helped him – all the knives in his hands became so blunt, one might think that they were brought from a restaurant... gradually, he elevated suicide attempts into an art. He made a big fire around himself with books by suicide writers: Hemingway, Mishima, Zweig, London and others, but it turned out that he sweated over it in vain. Then he tried to become an equilibrist and walked along a rope thrown over a large canyon without a safety net, but he kept his balance so perfectly that he could not fall. Even the fact that he supported Manchester United and then took up the translation of Musil into Hindi did not help him... Atticus began to lose his patience – when you are perfect, you want to be perfect in everything.

But he couldn't commit suicide.

Chapter 10 – The Author's Confession

"Damn it!" Memento Mori was tired of sitting idle. "What shall we do now?"

"I think I figured out the penultimate coordinate," Matthew seemed to have taken advantage of the break more fruitfully. His mind was enlightened at the time of the forty-seventh sunset, and now he waited only for Memento Mori's approval. "In that chapter... well, the one with the ads, you know... almost every poster had a number written on it... anyway, I thought that maybe the desired part of the coordinate is the sum of their addition."

"Oh, how I'm tired of wandering back and forth in this book!" Memento Mori sighed semi-theatrically and tried to hide his joy at the persuasiveness of Matthew's version. "I'll go and at least check it out..."

A few seconds after the disappearance of Memento Mori, there came the sound of footsteps from the middle of the planet.

"How could you check it so soon?" Matthew turned round in surprise.

But it wasn't Memento Mori.

Matthew felt his heart beat with a terrible force.

"Aloha!" Leah greeted him with a wave of her hand, and as it seemed to him, smiled warmly at him. "I think I even missed you..."

"...The Author turned out to be not so terrible as I thought. Apparently, he is an ordinary fellow. He confessed to me that he had kidnapped me in order to justify his digressing into another genre, and he broke up with poor Professor Arno because he was tired of writing four polylogues for characters." Leah began to tell her story after Memento Mori returned. "He whined all the time that it seemed to him that he was just having fun with this book, putting emphasis on form rather than content, and that he had nothing serious to say. As a result, people can say that his previous book was better, or be surprised – how it happened that for four years he wasn't able to write anything more interesting. Sometimes when he came up with something about you, he let me read it and asked me how convincing it all sounded, or if there was anything superfluous so that it wouldn't come out empty blah blah... in the end, I was so tired of his endless whining that one fine day I took advantage of his departure for work, and wrote the beginning of this chapter myself, so that I would return to you..."

"So the idea of adding up the numbers on the billboards was yours?" Matthew got sad.

"Yes. I had more time to think while you were demanding doves from heaven."

"Did you read that chapter too?" Matthew didn't know where to put himself, but then thought that in that idiotic book he could really put himself anywhere by chance, and changed his mind about using this idiom.

"Not only read it, but gave it a title too," Leah said, and again it seemed to Matthew that she smiled at him warmly.

"In my opinion, you forgot that we have to save the world," Memento Mori broke the idyll by waving a sheet of coordinates. "Besides, I don't quite believe in the amiability of those Authors who turn out to be *not so terrible, but very ordinary fellows*.

Nothing good can be expected from someone who sacrifices a character because of the difficulty of writing dialogue... so, it's high time to leave. Did you change anything else in this chapter?"

"Nothing significant," Leah felt ashamed. "I wrote the ending as well. But it doesn't concern us, and I'll just leave it for me to read."

"As you wish," Memento Mori did not insist as Leah could take it as a moral abuse against her, and besides, he himself could read everything without her permission. Therefore, he simply entered the coordinates of the last point into the time machine and a few minutes later disappeared from the planet along with his companions.

After twenty-two sunsets, a child in a green robe and a red bow appeared on the planet. "It's good that the tedious journey is over. I don't understand. How can this place be exchanged for that terrible and huge ball?" he said. "These adults are really weird..."

A Bit More about the Planet Kimkardash

Referendums are very popular in Kimkardash. The first referendum was held here just on the issue of whether it was necessary to resolve all topical issues through referendums. Since then, referendums have been held on all issues: should local losers be banned from impersonating geniuses on Earth; whether mass teleportation should be introduced if it contributes to increasing the obesity rate among Kimkardashians; is it necessary to continue using large-scale fireworks and illuminations on holidays in the hope that Earthlings will still consider them to be the northern lights, etc.

However, one of the most memorable referendums in the history of Kimkardash was held when the local scientists developed the formula for predicting the future. "Do you want to know in advance everything about your life from birth to death in the smallest detail, so that you can change it if necessary?" – that was the very simple question posed by the referendum, and the answer to it was also supposed to be simple, such as "Of course!" or "Why not?"

But it turned out quite differently. The votes were divided exactly into two. "The future will belong to those who own it," said one half of the population. "And how do we know that by changing something we will prevent a disaster? Maybe the disaster will be caused due to the changes we will make?" the other half argued. "A society that lives only with the future will not have a great future," they added.

As a result, the project failed. "We knew it," the learned prophets reassured themselves, and decided to try their achievements on Earthlings, as on guinea pigs. The book in which they planned to describe the future of the Earth had to be both tangible and inaccessible, something like the fruit of the Tree of Knowledge.

What Else Is There Left?
Latitude – SPOILER[43] 1'17" N. Longitude – 125°44'0" E. Year 2035[44]

"Where are we?"

They stood in a large square. It was raining in about the same way as in the decisive scenes of action films. You could see old multi-storey buildings with eight, nine or even ten floors all around, but nobody had any time, desire or reason to check the exact number of those floors. Neither did the Author himself, who wasted much more time on writing these long sentences explaining why they hadn't counted the floors than he would on counting them. But it was not so important anyway. Important was the thirty-three-storey building that stood out among other buildings like a badly inserted figure in Tetris, or the neck of a sanguine giraffe between the choleric alpacas.[45] On one side of the building was a huge mosaic portrait of the Leader. Four windows were carved on the portrait – two instead of pupils of his eyes and two instead of his nostrils. The eyes were the

---

43 **Spoiler** – if you haven't noticed this part of the latitude yet, you can find it in the comic chapter.

44 **manual** – enter these coordinates on the website – https://www.gps-coordinates.net/ – and you yourself will find the only non-simulated place on Earth.

45 **Sanguine giraffe between the choleric alpacas** – the types of temperaments in this sentence do not matter, nor do the alpacas. In general, even this simile itself, like everything else in the world, does not matter.

windows of the Leader's office, from where he could watch, if not the whole city, then most of it. There were punishment rooms at the nostrils, and from time to time, enemies of the Kimkardashian project would fly down from the windows. Residents called these events *runny nose* or *sneezing* of the Leader, and even said *bless you* to those who, after flying twenty floors, no longer cared.

"If I'm not mistaken, this is a **SPOILER**," said Memento Mori.

He was right. Kimkardashian scientists chose the perfect place for their experiments. At first, while the channels of communication were being established and the world was becoming globalised, they did not pay much attention to conspiracies. In those days, the territory was either part of a large empire, or passed into the hands of the allies after the war; and at times it even was absolutely independent.

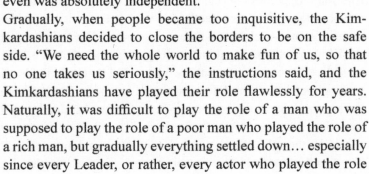

Gradually, when people became too inquisitive, the Kimkardashians decided to close the borders to be on the safe side. "We need the whole world to make fun of us, so that no one takes us seriously," the instructions said, and the Kimkardashians have played their role flawlessly for years. Naturally, it was difficult to play the role of a man who was supposed to play the role of a poor man who played the role of a rich man, but gradually everything settled down... especially since every Leader, or rather, every actor who played the role of the Leader was also from Kimkardash.

Issuing absurd laws wasn't difficult either: it was forbidden to stand with one's back to the monument of the Leader, and therefore, when taking a photo at the monument, people stood with their backs to the photographer; it was forbidden to fly to the sun without a visa; to use the words God and Leader in one sentence in order to avoid tautology; it was forbidden to read books by Authors whose first names were not Kim (the only exception was one of the novels of a certain old Author, Rudyard Kipling); high-ranking officials could not close their eyes in public places (except when they could not help but sneeze), and so on.

However, these laws were in effect only when it was necessary for the "rest of the world" to know about them. So, with the help of specially embedded guides, tourists learned about them only on the condition that they would not tell anyone anywhere anything about them, since this was a 100% guarantee that the news of this would reach the rest of the world at the first opportunity.

The Leader took a deep breath. He was fed up with these role-playing games. At one time he even thought about death, or about faking his own death, and let someone else, with the name of someone else, do whatever he wished. But he knew that the Kimkardashians would never forgive him for that. While he was alive, he had to assure the whole world that only the local people lived in the simulated reality and not them. To determine the approximate duration of the experiment, the Leader decided to review the news. "All of this seems like it will be over very soon," he thought, "the world is getting more and more crazy." The Leader certainly had reason to come to that conclusion.

Only the post-vegetarian movement was quite enough – the generation following the vegetarians and claiming that all food had a spirit. Therefore, they preferred to starve to death than to kill the souls of food. The number of post-vegetarians grew every day, but thanks to the diligence of veteran activists, it simultaneously decreased daily. The committees for saving the languages of the world also fought tirelessly, because due to political correctness it was becoming increasingly difficult to come up with such phrases that would not infringe the interests, honour and dignity of some group – be it agnostic monkeys who were forcibly transferred from Africa to Asia, people, who despite overfeeding, still did not gain weight, twins born under the sign of pisces, white-skinned children running in the snow, or someone else. Therefore, fearing public cyberbullying caused by an incorrectly uttered phrase, people almost stopped speaking and the danger of the degeneration of languages grew day by day. **The scientists who remained idle having invented everything, began to create a thousand nonsenses. For example, they tried to make robots that would then make people; they also worked on creating models of virtual hell and paradise, which later were to replace the prison and pension system.** Special psychological courses were appointed for those who did not walk in the streets looking at their mobile phones and expressed a desire to talk when they met friends. **To gain popularity in social networks, the President of the United States one day acted as a fireman, next day as a policeman, and then even as a construction worker. So, he had no time to be the President.** A lack of time was a serious problem for most people, so they installed in their mobile phones a special chip with downloaded series that they could watch in their sleep as an ordinary dream… **one of the popular publications even wrote about two of the latest scandals: the first was that people had deciphered Kimkardashian's most successful scheme for observing them – cats! All cats on Earth were actually hidden cameras that people brought home at will. Naturally, no one would have suspected the Kimkardashians, since they had no idea of their existence. But the collapse of the method tested for centuries still turned out to be unpleasant.** The second scandal concerned the world of advertising. The journalist revealed one of the creative agencies, saying that they even invented an entire country in Africa to get prizes at advertising awards. They ran various campaigns along with hired actors of colour. They either lured thick-boned tourists to that fake country to save the population of plump lions, or taught representatives of pseudo-primitive tribes how to communicate with the outside world using emojis.

"What's the point of keeping such a world?" thought the Leader and was just about to come up with another absurd law when someone broke into his office by kicking the door. The door was already open and Memento Mori could enter the office freely, but in his opinion, kicking the door would add piquancy to the final episode.

"Who are you and how did you get here?" asked the bewildered Leader. As a rule, it was necessary to go through several barriers to get to his office. But when he noticed a caricature superhero among three people, he guessed that something unusual was happening.

"We are looking for a book that describes the future of

mankind, and will not allow the apocalypse to happen," Memento Mori got straight to the point so that the reader would not waste time.

The Leader himself did not want to allow the apocalypse until the moment when the scientists of Kimkardash ordered it. "I'm not going to say even under torture that both the book and the button will appear at the pronunciation of the word "inferno", the Leader thought admiring his own courage, since he had no idea about the supernatural gift of Memento Mori. But when he came to know about it, it was already too late.

"Inferno!" Memento Mori pronounced in a firm voice, and at the same moment a secret niche opened behind them.

"The desire to know one's own future is always fatal," said the Leader. "You can touch anything in this office, except for the book. If you open the book, humanity will have to start from scratch.[46]

---

46 **The beginning of the end** – there are no perfect endings. Some think that a Happy End is the safest way out; others will never open a book again if the book has an unhappy ending; some don't like it if you explain everything to them and do not leave anything that the reader must work out; if the ending is not entirely clear, you will be criticised and asked what you meant by that. Therefore, this book will have two endings. The instruction is very simple – leave the ending that you like more, and just forget the second one.

***

The alarm clock rang at exactly four thirty-three.

"Another five minutes and I'll ge…" began Death, but right in the middle of the sentence suddenly remembered the importance of his task and got up before he finished the phrase. He should no longer make a mistake. He turned off the alarm clock, put on his cloak and sat down at the ATROPOS right when the secret niche opened up in the Leader's office. At the same moment, the story became parallel, since Memento Mori could not be in two places simultaneously.

The instruction was very simple. Death stretched. He was enjoying the last seconds of relaxation that were left before his next holidays. He was already fed up with the whole of humanity and their senseless ambitions. "Before everything starts over, I should get a good night's sleep," he thought. The Kimkardashians promised him that they would only once have another try, and if they still did not find the ideal model for the development of the Earth, they would certainly stop

Memento Mori opened the book very carefully right on the last page. There was only one sentence written there: **Do not push the red button**. "Is that all?" he was surprised. "Have we really gone through one hundred and seventy-something pages only to not push that button? What should we do – go back and wait until some madman who is angry at life decides to blow up the whole world?" But Memento Mori didn't have to wait long. While he was struggling with their project. "I must endure it one more time," Death tried to cheer himself up. "One big cycle…" However, it took a very long time for the first living things to begin to form from the first cells, longer than many millennia. A million-year-holiday.

"Stop, moment," Death whispered, "You are wonderful!"

A red light switched on along the ATROPOS. It was about five. **Hasta la vista**, he thought, marked all the folders and then, extremely pleased, pressed the phalanx of his index finger on the *Delete* to start all over again.

the disappointment caused by the banal ending, Atticus appeared on the doorstep. "I'll still kill myself if I have to blow up the whole world for that!" He announced confidently, crossed the room and, while Memento Mori thought what a strange sense of humour ideal people had, and while Leah wondered when the Author would tell Matthew that she was in love with him too, Atticus pushed the red button. "Houston, we have a problem," Memento Mori gasped.

…And then there was an explosion.
A Big Bang.

***

A single sentence was written in a thousand-page book: **Do not push the red button!**

"If that's the only thing that needs to be done to prevent the Apocalypse, I don't think any of us would want to touch that button…" Matthew said. "But if someone still tries to do it, he will first have to kill me!"

"I wish you didn't watch those stupid films!" Memento Mori shook his head. Nor could he believe that everything would not end by not pressing the button.

And it didn't.

Just as those in the room were struggling with the disappointment caused by the banal ending, Atticus appeared on the doorstep. "I'll still kill myself if I have to blow up the whole world for that!" he announced spotting the red button, and since he too, had been watching those stupid films, guessed that pushing that button at the end of the book would cause a serious disaster.

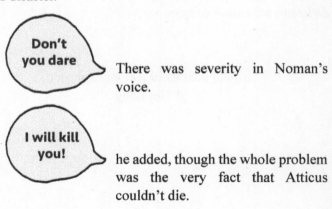

There was severity in Noman's voice.

he added, though the whole problem was the very fact that Atticus couldn't die.

And Memento Mori realised that even if the whole Kimkardash tried to protect the red button, they would not be able to resist the perfect character.

"I know what to do," he whispered to Matthew. "I'll run away, and you try to stop him. I need time to get to the first pages."

"How can I stop him?" Matthew was confused.

"I don't know... make him talk about his childhood, how he grew up, what psychological trauma he suffered, what colours he likes, where he sees himself in five years, or ask him to give you the opportunity to call your mother... in short, come up with something! Meanwhile, I could manage to go through twenty pages, at least."

And Memento Mori disappeared.

"Atticus," Matthew began, "you're the perfect person, and the perfect person must be able to admit that he's not always perfect. I understand that you're in trouble now, but that's the way the world works – if you want to leave traces, then you have to walk in mud first. You can't destroy all of humanity just because you had a nightmare or oversalted a dish. We are approaching our end every day. With our carelessness, we are destroying relationships built over the years and erect multistory buildings in order to deprive our children of the sky – the most beautiful invention in the world. We buy and buy cars that we do not need like air, and think that the efforts of one person will not change anything. We know that we need to live as if it's our last day, but we live as if it's the last day of the universe, not valuing nature at all. It doesn't matter whether you push the button now or years from now, because destruction is inevitable anyway. It's just that if you don't do it now, we will have a chance to enjoy the remaining few seconds in this world where you can still find a person..."

"Well, then you can enjoy the few seconds it takes me to get to the button from here," smiled Atticus, pushing Noman away with one blow and moving towards the button.

"Can you tell me about your childhood first?" Matthew tried to use the last chance. But it was too late – Atticus pushed the button...

...Having hung his cloak over the electric chair, Death began to think about coveted holidays. He really deserved a good rest after millions of years without a single day off. "Of course, *He* doesn't care... *He* himself rests on Sundays, anyway", Death grumbled, and suddenly spotted someone in the dark... damned hallucinations! He rubbed his eye sockets with finger phalanges and scrutinised the darkness in front of him. This time he saw no one there, as Memento Mori had already hidden away. Now he simply had to wait until Death would have fallen asleep and then switch off the alarm clock...

...And then there was no Big Bang! There was nothing. Atticus threw himself out of the window in desperation. If at that moment some Kimkardashian had stood at the building, he would have seen how a figure that looked like a teardrop rolled down from the eyes of the Mosaic Image of the Leader, how it flew twenty-five floors, crashed to the ground and immediately got up with the firm intention of finding refuge in another book, getting married, having two children and starting from scratch...

"...A disaster once averted does not rule out danger," Matthew noted.

"Certainly," replied Memento Mori. They were standing

in the same place – Leah's apartment – from where they had previously set off on a trip. "Although," he added, "in a novel with only two paragraphs left, you are unlikely to be in danger. Live in peace. No Big Brother will be able to watch you anymore."

"And you?" Tears welled up in Leah, but it seemed too banal to her to cry when saying goodbye.

"Umm… there are so many books and so little time, you know. And there are still a thousand characters to be saved…" said Memento Mori and disappeared. Without saying goodbye. Like Holden Caulfield, or Griffin, or the Cheshire Cat. He hated sentimental scenes, and in his haste, forgot to mention that in the rest of their life together he would never see Leah and Matthew again; that he couldn't warn Noman not to go back to the comic, because Big-ear Joe was waiting for him in the very first illustration; and he couldn't tell Matthew that the Author hinted at his life together with Leah in the middle of this paragraph. So, the only thing Matthew said was:

"Wait a minute, and what shall we do with this caricature Noman?"

***

Death woke up at eleven fifty-nine. He hadn't slept so sweetly for ages. He knew he couldn't avoid the Kimkardashians' anger, and therefore decided to sleep longer while he had time. So he rolled over and continued to sleep.

No one died on Earth that day.

Beka Adamashvili

Recommended Reading

If you have enjoyed reading *Everbody dies in this Novel* you should also like Beka Adamashvili's first novel *Bestseller* and the postmodernist novels of Andrew Crumey and Jean-Pierre Ohl as well as the novels of Robert Irwin:

Pfitz – Andrew Crumey
D'Alembert's Principle – Andrew Crumey
Mr Mee – Andrew Crumey
Mobius Dick – Andrew Crumey
The Secret Knowledge – Andrew Crumey
Mr Dick or The Tenth Book – Jean-Pierre Ohl
The Lairds of Cromarty – Jean-Pierre Ohl
The Arabian Nightmare – Robert Irwin
The Limits of Vision – Robert Irwin
Exquisite Corpse – Robert Irwin
Satan Wants Me – Robert Irwin

These books can be bought from your local bookshop, online from your favourite internet bookseller or direct from Dedalus. Please write to Cash Sales, Dedalus Limited, 24-26, St Judith's Lane, Sawtry, Cambs, PE28 5XE. For further details of the Dedalus list please go to our website: www.dedalusbooks.com or write to us for a catalogue or email: info@dedalusbooks.com

Pfitz – AndrewCrumey

'Rreinnstadt is a place which exists nowhere – the conception of a 18th century prince who devotes his time, and that of his subjects, to laying down on paper the architecture and street-plans of this great, yet illusory city. Its inhabitants must also be devised: artists and authors, their fictional lives and works, all concocted by different departments. When Schenck, a worker in the Cartography Office, discovers the "existence" of Pfitz, a manservant visiting Rreinnstadt, he sets about illicitly recreating Pfitz's life. Crumey is a daring writer: using the stuff of fairy tales, he ponders the difference between fact and fiction, weaving together philosophy and fantasy to create a magical, witty novel.'   *The Sunday Times*

'*Pfitz* is a surprisingly warm and likeable book, a combination of intellectual high-wire act and good traditional storytelling with a population of lovers and madmen we do care about, despite their advertised fictionality. Certainly, Crumey's narrative gymnastics have not affected his ability to create strong, fleshy characters, and none more fleshy, more fleshly, than Frau Luppen, Schenck's middle-aged landlady, a great blown rose of a woman who express her affection for her lodger by feeding him bowls of inedible stew.'

Andrew Miller in *The New York Times*

'Built out of fantasy, Andrew Crumey's novel stands, like the monumental museum at the centre of its imaginary city, as an edifice of erudition.'

Andrea Ashworth in *The Times Literary Supplement*

£8.99 ISBN 978 1 909232 80 8 146p B. Format

Mr Dick or The Tenth Book – Jean-Pierre Ohl

'Mr Dick is a character from *David Copperfield* and Ohl's book is in many ways a homage to Dickens. It is the story of two young Frenchmen whose lives are consumed by their obsession with Dickens' life and books and in particular his final, unfinished novel, *The Mystery of Edwin Drood*. It's a playful and highly literary detective story, like a Gallic mélange of *Flaubert's Parrot* by Julian Barnes and AS Byatt's *Possession*.'   Sam Taylor in *The Observer*

'…a wonderfully inventive story of a feud between two French Drood scholars, interposed with the unreliable journal of a young Frenchman who visits Dickens just before he dies.'
                              Andrew Taylor in *The Independent*

'The narrative Jean-Pierre Ohl's novel is flashily post-modern in technique and reminiscent of Umberto Eco's *The Name of the Rose*.'   John Sutherland in *The Financial Times*

£9.99   ISBN   978 1 903517 68 0   224p   B. Format

The Arabian Nightmare – Robert Irwin

'Robert Irwin is indeed particularly brilliant. He takes the story-within-a-story technique of the Arab storyteller a stage further, so that a tangle of dreams and imaginings becomes part of the narrative fabric. The prose is discriminating and, beauty of all beauties, the book is constantly entertaining.'

Hilary Bailey in *The Guardian*

'Robert Irwin writes beautifully and is dauntingly clever but the stunning thing about him is his originality. Robert Irwin's work, while rendered in the strictest, simplest and most elegant prose, defies definition. All that can be said is that it is a bit like a mingling of *The Thousand and One Nights* and *The Name of the Rose*. It is also magical, bizarre and frightening.'

Ruth Rendell

'At one stage in this labyrinthine narrative, a character complains "things just keep coming round in circles". The form of this clever tale owes something to *The Thousand and One Nights*. The subject matter is exotic and Eastern, the episodes linked tangentially and mingling one into another. Into the thread of the stories, Irwin injects discussions on sexuality and religion. However, since dreams, as we are shown, are themselves a deception, then the philosophical points must necessarily be falsehoods. The invention is exuberant, but the author manages to keep control to stop everything lurching into shapeless indulgence. The result is a unique and challenging fantasy.'

The Observer

'...a classic orientalist fantasy tells the story of Balian of Norwich and his misadventures in a labyrinthine Cairo at the time of the Mamelukes. Steamy, exotic and ingenious, it is a boxes-within-boxes tale featuring such characters as Yoll, the Storyteller, Fatima the Deathly and the Father of Cats. It is a compelling meditation on reality and illusion, as well as on *Arabian Nights*-style storytelling. At its elusive centre lies the affliction of the Arabian Nightmare: a dream of infinite suffering that can never be remembered on waking, and might almost have happened to somebody else.'

Phil Baker in *The Sunday Times*

'Deft and lovely and harder to describe than to experience... the smooth steely grip of Irwin's real story-telling genius *The Arabian Nightmare* is a joy to read. If Dickens had lived to complete *The Mystery of Edwin Drood*, the full tale when told might have had something in common with the visionary urban dreamscape Robert Irwin has so joyfully unfolded in this book.'

John Clute in *The Washington Post*

£7.99 ISBN 978 1 873982 73 0 266p B. Format

Exquisite Corpse – Robert Irwin

'*Exquisite Corpse* is among the most adventurous, ambitious and daring novels published so far this decade.'

Nicholas Royle in *Time Out*

'Robert Irwin is a master of the surreal imagination. Historical figures such as Aleister Crowley and Paul Eluard vie with fictional characters in an extended surrealist game, which, like the movement itself, is full of astonishing insights and hilarious pretensions. Superb.'

Ian Critchley in *The Sunday Times*

'*Exquisite Corpse* is one of the best novels I have read by an English person in my reading time. When I first read it I was completely bowled over.'

A.S. Byatt on Radio 4's Saturday Review

'The final chapter of the novel reads like a realistic epilogue to the book, but may instead be a hypnogogic illusion, which in turn casts doubt on many other events in the novel. Is Caroline merely a typist from Putney or the very vampire of Surrealism? It's for the reader to decide.'

Steven Moore in *The Washington Post*

£8.99 ISBN 978 1 907650 54 3 249p B. Format

The beginning of *Bestseller* by Beka Adamashvili:

I

PR-Step
or
Oops! – Straight into Hell...

Pierre Sonnage firmly decided to commit suicide on his 33rd birthday. His motivation was not banal at all, I mean he hadn't caught his bride and the best man making love before the wedding; he hadn't gradually lost everything – his head, hopes and the last shirt – in a gambling house; he had never gone so deep into the existential problems as to be dragged into a swamp of vanity; neither was he seriously in debt to anyone except humankind for building a house, planting a tree and fathering a single son. In fact, when planning the suicide, its mission was far more idealistic than the mere prospect of solving the eternal dilemma of the immortality of the soul.

The thing is that Pierre Sonnage was a writer! Maybe unknown and not even socially active, but still. He belonged to the category of the creative individuals who prefer writing many books to reading them. Consequently, he had already published a lot of short stories and even four thick books. In some way he resembled Rubens for being fond of creating massive and heavy pieces. Nevertheless, literary gourmets rated his 'heavy' creations as 'easily digestible'. On the whole, the appraisal was not bad, but the rating didn't seem favourable to Pierre since standing on the same platform with Houellebecq, Le Clézio, and Beigbeder wasn't easy for him. Moreover, there were only a dozen readers at the presentation of his last book. True, he was not planning a grand presentation but we must admit that having a crowd of only twelve readers at the age of 33 is not a big number.

That, of course, could be explained easily: Pierre wholeheartedly believed that 'society was not ready to accept and appreciate his brilliant ideas'. So, in order to guide it to the true path, he had 'to take an effective step'. It was then that the idea of committing suicide, which gave rise to the whole complicated story, occurred to him…

(As Pierre Sonnage commits suicide at the end of this chapter, the Author did not consider it necessary to describe his appearance or personal traits at this point.)

Oh yes, Pierre decided to sacrifice himself to his creative life, as he knew that death has one immortal feature – it boosts respect.[1] Suicide was the only way for him to achieve eternal glory, because he knew another proven maxim[2] too: a man had to die to gain a deathless fame.

As one can commit suicide more or less only once in life, he wanted the event to happen with dignity and pomp. Therefore, he began to prepare for it far in advance. He refused to use the rope from the very start, since the rope which he had found in his closet was just as worn out as the method itself of committing suicide by hanging. He rejected the idea of shooting himself for the same reason (besides, he would die with fear before pulling the trigger). What's more important, he was absolutely sure that his brains deserved to be kept in a better place (say a glass container with a special liquid, proudly exposed in a museum) than on an ordinary wall. He even had thought of taking 33 sleeping pills, but later realised that after the autopsy nobody would be able to count the amount of the pills, and this smart symbolism would remain an eternal secret for the history of world literature. True, he could indicate it in his suicide note, but the sentence 'I'm 33 now, so I've decided to take 33 sleeping pills' would sound pretty odd, and he would rather die than write such rubbish!

There were myriads of other methods of committing suicide: demonstrative self-immolation in Rouen Square, jumping from the stream of life into the stream of the Seine, tasting raw fugu-fish, taking a loan from a bank or just jumping

---

1 He even wrote in one of his novels: 'If we showed our respect towards people as generously as we do posthumously, they would live a much longer and happier life.'

2 The Author could here use the synonymous words, such as 'truth', 'wisdom', 'axiom', etc. But as he is a maximalist, he decided to pretend to be more intellectual (note of the intel. Auth.)

under the train with his own books in his hand, thus attracting the passengers' attention with his aggressive advertising or with a desperate scream.

However, since Pierre believed that he contemplated the future standing on Newton's shoulders,[1] he decided to look death in the eye from a maximum height. Naturally, he rejected the moon and Everest at once; Everest because it was far away and the moon because it was even farther. Besides, even if his body was ever discovered, it was unlikely that anyone would considered a French writer who turned into a satellite or froze in the deep snows of Everest a suicide. So, with a cold mind and a warm heart, Pierre chose a height which he could reach quite easily.

Thus, on the day of his 33rd anniversary, he found himself in Dubai – the city built out of almost nothing – to build his own future out of almost nothing as well…

(Based on the fact that the Author hates depicting landscapes as his memory always delicately refuses to recall the beautiful words concerning the details of reliefs and bas-reliefs, he omits the description of any Dubai sights. As for the Burj Khalifa, it's easier to find its image on google than read its description which would take three pages at least.)

And lo, Pierre saw the Burj Khalifa with his own eyes, stepped into the lift with his own feet…

---

1 In order to prove that the Author's knowledge of the word "maxim" was not accidental, here he paraphrases the famous expression by Isaac Newton: 'If I have seen further than the others, it is by standing on the shoulders of giants.'